RAIDER UNLEASHED

BROTHERHOOD PROTECTORS WORLD

TEAM KOA: ALPHA

BOOK THREE

LORI MATTHEWS

Twisted Page Press LLC

For my readers.
I cherish each and every one of you. XO

ACKNOWLEDGMENTS

A huge thank you to my editor, Heidi Senesac. You are amazing. Thanks for making my work coherent. Another fantastic individual is my assistant, Sara Mallion. She makes everything so much easier and I would be lost without her.

My fellow writers, Janna MacGregor, Stacey Wilk, Kimberley Ash, and Tiara Inserto, are all truly amazing authors but even more, they're the friends that keep me grounded. Thank you ladies for always being there. My super supportive family also deserves a big thanks. They keep me laughing and make everyday better.

And last but not least; to you the reader. Your emails and posts mean so much. Thank you.

BROTHERHOOD PROTECTORS
ORIGINAL SERIES BY ELLE JAMES

Brotherhood Protectors Series

Montana SEAL (#1)

Bride Protector SEAL (#2)

Montana D-Force (#3)

Cowboy D-Force (#4)

Montana Ranger (#5)

Montana Dog Soldier (#6)

Montana SEAL Daddy (#7)

Montana Ranger's Wedding Vow (#8)

Montana SEAL Undercover Daddy (#9)

Cape Cod SEAL Rescue (#10)

Montana SEAL Friendly Fire (#11)

Montana SEAL's Mail-Order Bride (#12)

SEAL Justice (#13)

Ranger Creed (#14)

Delta Force Rescue (#15)

Dog Days of Christmas (#16)

Montana Rescue (#17)

Montana Ranger Returns (#18)

BROTHERHOOD PROTECTORS WORLD

ORIGINAL SERIES BY ELLE JAMES

Brotherhood Protectors Hawaii World

Team Koa Alpha

Lane Unleashed - Regan Black

Harlan Unleashed - Stacey Wilk

Raider Unleashed - Lori Matthews

Waylen Unleashed - Jen Talty

Kian Unleashed - Kris Norris

Brotherhood Protectors Yellowstone World

Team Wolf

Guarding Harper - - Desiree Holt

Guarding Hannah - Delilah Devlin

Guarding Eris - Reina Torres

Guarding Payton - Jen Talty

Guarding Leah - Regan Black

Team Eagle

Booker's Mission - Kris Norris

Hunter's Mission - Kendall Talbot

Gunn's Mission - Delilah Devlin

Xavier's Mission - Lori Matthews

Wyatt's Mission - Jen Talty

Corbin's Mission - Jen Talty

Tyson's Mission - Delilah Devlin

Knox's Mission - Barb Han

Colton's Mission - Kendall Talbot

Walker's Mission - Kris Norris

Brotherhood Protectors Colorado World

Team Watchdog

Mason's Watch - Jen Talty

Asher's Watch - Leanne Tyler

Cruz's Watch - Stacey Wilk

Kent's Watch- Deanna L. Rowley

Ryder's Watch- Kris Norris

Team Raptor

Darius' Promise - Jen Talty

Simon's Promise - Leanne Tyler

Nash's Promise - Stacey Wilk

Spencer's Promise - Deanna L. Rowley

Logan's Promise - Kris Norris

Team Falco

Fighting for Esme - Jen Talty

Fighting for Charli - Leanne Tyler

Fighting for Tessa - Stacey Wilk

Fighting for Kora - Deanna L. Rowley

Fighting for Fiona - Kris Norris

Athena Project

Beck's Six - Desiree Holt

Victoria's Six - Delilah Devlin

Cygny's Six - Reina Torres

Fay's Six - Jen Talty

Melody's Six - Regan Black

Team Trojan

Defending Sophie - Desiree Holt

Defending Evangeline - Delilah Devlin

Defending Casey - Reina Torres

Defending Sparrow - Jen Talty

Defending Avery - Regan Black

---

*P*iper Holloway gritted her teeth. She hated Stephen Wallis with a startling intensity, but she had to suck it up. His nickname was Slick which she had no doubt he'd given to himself but she thought of him more as Slug or Slimy.

"What do ya think, Pipe? You in?" Slug took a sip of his Starbucks. He was never without a cup in his hand. He was so caffeinated he could do the jitterbug standing still. She'd bumped into him one day and a bit spilled. From a tough-as-nails man, she'd thought the brew would be black as his demeanor, so she had been mildly shocked when something light and foamy spilled. Smelled more like vanilla and cinnamon than smoke and sin.

He shifted his weight and moved his feet in time to his caffeinated rhythm as he glanced around the decrepit parking garage. He tucked a gun in the waist band at the front of his jeans. Piper entertained herself by estimating the exact day and time he was going to shoot his balls off. Careless, especially with all his antsy movement from too much caffeine. She'd pay really literally anything to be there to witness the fallout.

Another thing… She hated being called Pipe. Just one more damn thing to add to the growing list of complaints about the slug in front of her. "Sure, I'm up for anything." She stood with her arms crossed over her chest and tried to keep her face neutral. Slug had a habit of glancing at her boobs and it pissed her off to no end. Honestly, the number of times she'd cleared her throat in conversation with him and pointed to her eyes was dumbfounding.

Slug grinned and clapped his hands. "That's what I told him. I knew you'd be in."

"Told who?" Unease shivered up her spine. When Slug had called, she debated not answering. The last thing she needed was to deal with him. History had taught her that he'd screw her over in a heartbeat. She sighed. He was also a guy with all the right connections, which meant she had to deal with him if she wanted to hit her goals.

The smile fell off his face. "It doesn't matter. He needed a driver and an extra set of hands. That's you." He pulled his phone out of his pocket and punched in what was probably a text. Within seconds, she received a text. "Did you text me?" she asked pulling out her phone.

Slug shook his head. "No. The boss did."

She glanced at the screen. Sweat broke out between her shoulder blades. "What is this? Is this a plane ticket?"

"Yup. You got three hours. You'd better hustle." Slug pushed off the wall pillar and started walking with a funky hop-step gait toward the stairwell.

A scream climbed her throat, followed closely by the same sickening panic that was residual from dealing with Slug. What had he gotten her into? What the fuck was she supposed to do? She didn't want to go anywhere, and three hours wasn't enough time to organize anything anyway.

She hollered after Slug. "Wait, what the hell is this? You never said I had to get on an airplane."

Slug danced around to face her with a grin. "What's the matter, Pipe? You afraid of flyin'?"

Flying was the least of her worries. "No, but I thought the job was here in San Diego." She tried to be calm, sound whiny even because there was no way she could let him in on the fact that she was now in a full-blown panic. It wasn't supposed to happen this way.

Slug grinned wickedly. "You thought wrong, baby."

That was it. A fast and furious urge to kill the slug rose within her. She wanted to pull the gun out of her pocket and cap the asshole. "You neglected to tell me it was out of town." She shrugged. "I don't know if I want to do it anymore."

Slug froze for an instant. He turned and started back toward her at a clip. He stopped directly in front of her. His expression was set in serious lines, like stick a penny in the crags and Lincoln's head might disappear. His eyes darted rapidly, but at least he wasn't looking at her tits. Small comfort considering the tight, flat slash that should be his mouth.

This close she realized Slug was much older than she thought. He had to be in his forties. He dressed and acted younger but the crevasses on his face said he had to be at least a decade older than her thirty-three. She'd never been this close to him before by design, and his nearness now was only solidifying her choice. Slug smelled. Fat man sweat, underlain with an acrid tang. Slug smelled of fear.

He growled, "You said you were up for anything. You said yes. You have to go. I told him you were going. You don't go and it won't be good for you, Piper. It'll be all bad. Very bad. Like deadly. And it won't be good for me either, so you get the fuck on that plane, you feel me?"

Slug's blue eyes were wide and his breath was coming in gasps. His pasty skin had gone paler which she didn't think was possible. The man in front of her wasn't just scared. He was terrified.

Her escalating pulse made it hard to catch a breath. "Who the hell is this job for? What the fuck have you gotten me into?" Piper demanded.

Beyond a shadow of a doubt, she was certain she knew who was behind it. Not his name, of course, but she knew who it was. The man she nicknamed the Snake had to be behind this curtain of secrecy. Had to be. He'd killed Marta and she would do anything to exact her revenge. For that reason alone, pushing aside her trepidations would be worth it. She wanted him to suffer before she killed him.

Slug leaned forward so they were almost nose to nose. "It don't matter who it is, you just make sure as fuck"—he poked her shoulder—"you are on that plane or we're both dead."

Piper swallowed convulsively, trying to avoid puking. This visceral reaction couldn't be the nearly overwhelming alarm ringing through her. Nope. It was Slug's putrid breath that was making her stomach revolt.

"Fine," she said as she brushed past him. "I'll be on the plane, but this is the last fucking time I'm answering your call, asshole." She went into the stairwell and ran down the three stories. Then turned left when she got to the street. The old green Passat she loved was parked at the curb. Getting in, she turned it over and pulled away from the curb just as Slug came out of the garage. She drove for another ten minutes trying to get her heart to climb down out of the stratosphere. Finally, she felt calm enough to pull over and pick up her cell. She dialed a number she knew by heart.

"Yeah," said the voice on the other end.

Overjoyed to share this snafu with someone else, Piper let out the breath she'd been holding. "We've got a major problem."

2

*R*aider Torres was in his version of paradise. Wasn't he the luckiest SOB in the world, to be standing in the headquarters building of the Brotherhood Protector's Hawaiian ranch, watching the monitor with a map of the Big Island on it? A familiar and welcome surge of adrenaline ran through his veins. He'd arrived on the Big Island of Hawai'i to attend his old commanding officer's retirement party.

Then a damn volcano erupted. The violent awakening was like heaven and Christmas all rolled into one. Okay, not for those people affected by it, but damn if he wasn't stoked. He needed action and Kilauea had just given him the excuse to get involved.

Jace Hawkins stood at the front of the room

and explained the situation. "Kilauea usually flows down into the water but this time, she's decided to do something different." Hawk pointed to the map. "These small towns on the perimeter of the island are in jeopardy. First responders are few and far between. Roads, too." He pointed out the hospitals, a couple of clinics, and the fire stations. Before he could say more, the radio crackled with the first calls for help. Fire. Injury. Smoke and ash.

Hawk cocked his head. "That's all southwest of us. These towns can get cut off in a hurry. The ash cloud alone can pose serious health problems and choke vehicles. As the calls for help come in, I'm gonna assign them." He pointed to a table of radios. "Grab one of those and the keys to a vehicle. Be sure your safety gear goes with you. Stay in contact with us here. We can coordinate more help if you need it. Just do what you can to evacuate folks from the danger zone. We'll keep you informed about the location of emergency shelters, if and when they open."

Raider fed off the energy in the room. Retirement sucked balls. He hated it. He was alone and bored ninety percent of the time. He'd been traveling with his team, his brothers in arms but it still didn't cut it. If one more person told him he just needed a hobby, he was going to blow like

Kilauea. Hobbies typically meant sitting still for long periods. Like fishing? What the heck was the appeal of that? Even as a Navy man, the idea of dropping a line in the water and sitting like a bump... Raider shuddered and refused to contemplate the hours of inactivity that came with that particular hobby. *Hmm, maybe mountain climbing.* Half Dome might be fun to scale. Once.

What he needed was a new job. Being a SEAL had been his life. Retirement was like losing a limb. Suddenly, like so many of the military's elite special ops, when retirement sank its deadly boring claws into them, he had no clue who he was or what he was supposed to do. His identity was as a member of a team. This going solo crap was for the birds. It had been six long months of trying to kill time.

He'd only survived because of his SEAL buddies, Lane, Harlan, Waylen, and Kian. They'd all retired at the same time which was the smartest thing any of them had ever done. Raider didn't think any single one of them would survive retirement on his own.

He glanced over the group. Waylen Brown, their resident tech geek who was really anything but was watching the screen intently. Raider knew his buddy was already assessing what would have to be done to keep comms running.

Lane Benning, who stood over Waylen's shoulder, was the best damn sniper ever. He used to tease Lane that his eyes were worth their weight in gold. Lane had saved their asses more times than Raider could count, and he knew Lane was studying the screen intently to see all the angles even though it wasn't necessarily warranted for a retirement party. But for an eruption? Yeah, maybe.

"Where are the MASH units going to be set up?" Kian Fox was already charting his route and asking about EMS and medical response.

Every team had personnel with medical training, and that was Kian. He'd seen Kian conduct a buddy transfusion, sending blood from his arm right into the veins of a gravely wounded sailor. All while bullets and rockets were flying over their heads. Bravest, coldest son of a bitch around. Raider would've sworn the man slept with his medical bag as a pillow.

Raider's best friend, Harlan Fender leaned toward him with a grunt. "Can you believe this shit? What are the chances that we'd be here for a volcanic eruption?"

Raider grinned. "About as much as you having a one-night stand so maybe there's still hope for you, buddy." They'd been ribbing Harlan about having a one-nighter before the volcano erupted. Harlan just wasn't that guy. Made Raider like him that much more. The guy had standards and he didn't break them. Not for anyone. He lived by his moral code, and he'd die by it and that was good with him.

As Hawk handed out jobs in the front, Raider fed off the energy surging through his body. This was a chance to be useful again.

He looked past his buddies and his gaze fell on Glenn Gadsden. He'd been a hell of a leader. They'd all gone to hell and back together for him and he'd always had their backs. The man looked happy but Raider couldn't be sure it wasn't an act. Picturing Gadsden sitting back and doing nothing didn't compute. Maybe he'd ask his old boss what the hell the secret to surviving retirement really was.

One of Raider's strengths was that he excelled at pretending. He'd spent the first part of the party chatting with the world, smiling and being all personable, as if he absolutely loved being here. Well shit, he did like Hawai'i. The little he'd seen of Waimea was amazing. The Big Island with everything from farmland to rainforest and black sandy beaches was one of the best stops they'd made.

Beside him, Lane tensed. He glanced at his buddy and then at the woman on the screen in the front of the room. Lane was already volunteering to help her. She was fine lookin'. No flies on Lane.

He grabbed a radio and a set of keys, and then he was gone.

Raider tucked his hands in his jeans pockets and waited to be assigned something. Anything. Hawk called Harlan's name and was talking about knocking on doors to alert people to the need to evacuate. Raider decided this was as good a job as any and followed along behind his friend. They grabbed radios and Harlan scooped up a set of keys and they hurried from the building.

The sky to the south was on fire. A stunning sight, but there was no time to gawk at it. People were in trouble. Volcanoes weren't something he was all that knowledgeable about, but he thought they usually gave more warning. Raider asked Harlan as much as he climbed into the passenger side.

Harlan shrugged as he got behind the wheel of a dark blue pickup. "I guess it's Mother Nature and she can sure be a cranky witch when she wants to be."

"Right?" Raider opened a map on his phone of the area where they were headed. "Got to say this is unexpected but it's a damn sight better than lounging on a beach all fucking day tomorrow."

Harlan grinned. "You gotta learn to relax."

"I've been relaxing. It's all I've been fuckin' doing. I can't take any more relaxation." Raider sighed.

"I hear that. Retirement has sucked balls."

"At least now we get to do something, although I gotta say, I'm liking the Big Island. I like the vibe. Hopefully, the volcano won't erupt for too long. Hate to see all the damage happen."

Raider shook his head. He was done dealing with this homeowner. Maude Turner didn't want to leave her house. She'd lived there for forty years and figured she'd survived other eruptions and she'd be just fine. When Harlan had pushed the issue she'd screamed and hollered, waving her arms in the air. Retirement hadn't slowed their reflexes too much. They both ducked when she'd hurled an ashtray at them.

That was when Raider gave up, leaving Harlan with the very upset elderly lady. He was much better with people than Raider was when it came to shit like this. Raider leaned against Officer Kalani's police cruiser, as Harlan walked toward him.

"She's packing as we speak." Harlan waggled his jaw and probed his cheek as he approached. He hauled in a deep breath. "It's never the ones you think who are the most trouble. She can't weigh more than a hundred pounds soaking wet and she's older than dirt, but she's got a hell of a mean right hook."

"I don't know how you do it. I don't have the patience to argue with them. It's logic. Get out and be safe." He held up his hands as if weighing something. "Stay and possibly die. I wanted to throw the last couple over my shoulder and dump them in the back of the police car and I would've left this one"—he indicated the house in front of them with his chin—"to the volcano." He straightened, brushing some ash off his shirt. It was getting thick. Kilauea wasn't letting up. All that lava was still pouring out.

"That's why you blow things up, instead," Harlan said as punched Raider in the shoulder.

"Officer Kalani's over there," Raider pointed to the house next door. "Other than the feather-weight golden gloves in there, these people are leaving. I'm hearing reports of traffic snarls on the radio. I'm gonna go direct traffic for a while. One accident and everything will be backed up for miles."

"Okay. Do you want me to swing by and pick you up when I'm leaving the area?"

"Nah, I'll find my own way. Stay in touch, though." The last thing Raider needed was for one of the team to get hurt now. They'd survived hell and to get hurt over a volcano would be just wrong on so many levels.

"Will do," Harlan said and started toward the next house.

"Hey, Fender… Meg'll be fine."

Harlan looked over his shoulder and nodded but as Raider watched his buddy walk away, his gut knotted. Harlan would be all twisted about not being able to go home to his sister Meg. There was nothing Raider could do but he felt the other man's anxiety over it. Worrying about family sucked sometimes. Okay, all of the time.

He made his way from the neighborhood toward the main road and started walking. He only made it a few blocks before he realized traffic wasn't moving at all. The sound of horns was deafening. The traffic lights at most intersections were out. People were yelling at each other through their car windows, cursing and raising their fists. Others were trying to edge their way through. It was one clown short of a circus. Oh wait, there was a clown who seemed to think he could drive over the sidewalk to get around everyone else. Raider held back a scoff of disgust when he spied a pile of guys on bikes on the corner blocking the clown's forward momentum.

With a silent curse, Raider assessed the situation with his usual military precision. His tolerance for people's bullshit was already in the red zone. The old beat-up gray Honda was the problem. It was blocking the lane and the guy who wanted to turn left into it was hung up in the intersection. Things appeared to have gone down-hill from there.

Raider took a deep breath and hurried between the vehicles. He approached the gray car and immediately understood the issue. The car was covered in ash and by the looks of things was totally dead. He glanced inside to find a woman and three small children along with all kinds of stuff packed to the roof line.

"Fuck me," he muttered.

It was probably their whole lives or as much as they could fit in the old car. He tapped on the window. The woman stared at him, her eyes huge and blinking. *Shit.* It was the one time in his life he wished he had a badge. Instead, he squatted on his haunches a few feet back from the window and gestured for her to lower it. She finally did so.

"Hey," Raider said with a smile. "The car won't start?"

She nodded and bit her lip.

He surveyed the area for possible options. The entrance to a strip mall parking lot was just half a block down. If he could push it there, he could solve the traffic snarl. He stood and looked around. "Let me see if I can find some help. We'll push you to that parking lot, okay?"

She nodded again as one of the little ones in

the back coughed. She immediately rolled up the window.

Raider looked around. He made eye contact with the guy in the truck behind the gray car and walked over. The window was already down and the guy's scowl was darker than the ash-clogged sky.

"You up for helping me push her out of the way?" Raider asked as he pointed to the car.

The man nodded and exited his truck. He was big, which was good because they were going to need all the help they could get. That small car was jammed full.

Others soon realized what was going on and joined them. Within minutes, a group of eight volunteers managed to get the car pushed down the street and into the parking lot. The drivers filtered back to their cars and the traffic started to move.

Raider knew it was only a matter of time with the lights out before it got all balled up again, but he decided to take a moment and go into the convenience store at the end of the strip mall and buy a bottle of water.

He turned to the woman in the car. "Are you going to be okay?"

She nodded. "My husband is on the way. He'll be here soon and fix the car. He knows what's wrong with it. He's a mechanic."

"Good. Okay. I'm going to the store. Do you need anything? For you or your kids?"

The little guy in the back of the car coughed again. She glanced back at him as she shook her head no. Then she started putting the window back up. "Thank you again," she said and then closed the window completely.

Raider started into the store. He didn't blame the woman. Anyone with asthma was in big trouble in this. He knew he was breathing in too much ash as it was, and he didn't have any lung issues. He entered the store and nodded to the guy behind the cash register as he went down the aisle to the back where the fridges were. He pulled out a large bottle of water and headed back toward the front. He stopped halfway when he spied a bunch of bandanas hanging on a rack. It wasn't a mask but it would do. He needed to stop breathing in so much ash. The only colors the guy had were red, blue, and black. Raider grabbed a black one and continued to the front. Last thing he wanted was for someone to mistake him as being affiliated with a gang.

"Hey," he said to the man behind the cash.

"Getting rough out there," the guy said. He was an inch or two shorter than Raider, with blond hair that was cut close to his head. His eyes were dark and his mouth had a twist to it. The guy gave off a vibe Raider wasn't loving, but it didn't matter much. He wasn't planning on chatting with the guy for long. Raider handed over the money for both the water and the bandana and then grabbed his change.

As he turned to go the door opened and the bell sounded. He looked up and found himself face-to-face with his ex-wife.

he glow in the sky only got brighter as Piper stared out the window. A fucking volcano. That's what had screwed everything up. A fucking volcano. It was unbelievable. Truly. She shifted her weight, trying to keep her ass from falling asleep.

She studied the back of the strip mall. A convenience store, a t-shirt shop, a sandwich place, two empty stores, and a bank. The only thing open was the convenience store, not that she could see it from there. Smart people were getting out of Dodge. Not only was it nighttime but there was a fucking volcano erupting not that far away.

Come on, come on. What the fuck were they doing in there that was taking so long? She was only here on a scouting mission. Nothing more tonight. The plan wasn't to do anything until tomorrow. This was just supposed to be them casing the place.

She glanced around but the back of the strip mall was blocked from view by palm tree foliage. Damn good thing, since her sitting in the van stick out like a sore thumb. It had been okay while traffic was snarled to a stop. But then it cleared up. Now, anyone with any sense was inside away from all the ash, not hanging out in their vehicle like a sitting duck. She adjusted her mask and looked across the van through the passenger side window at the steel door that was sealed up tighter than Fort Knox.

She'd been here too long. They were supposed to go in and spend ten maybe fifteen minutes. She glanced at her watch. Thirty-eight minutes. They just had to make sure they knew where to set everything up for tomorrow. That's it. What the hell was taking them so long? *Shit.* Every sense she had was on alert…this situation was fucked beyond repair.

Hang on! Signs of life had surfaced.

The steel door to one of the vacant stores opened and four men filed out. One was stumbling. Not good. Denlo had his ball cap pulled down low over his face and his jacket collar pulled up. The other two were half-carrying, half-dragging the third guy. He pulled open the back door. "We need to get water at the convenience store." He gestured to her to get out of the van.

"What the fuck?" she mumbled as she got out. Getting water didn't require two of them. She just wanted to be out of there. There'd been a huge issue with traffic before. She'd barely made it into the lot before the whole intersection became gridlocked.

They walked around to the front of the convenience store and Piper pulled the door open. She started in and almost walked straight into the man coming out. She looked up and cursed.

Raider?

Why was her ex-husband here? Standing right in front of her. She froze and Denlo plowed into her.

Raider reached out to catch her, but she jerked her arm away and gave him the tiniest head shake. He'd always been good at reading her body language, so he dropped his hand. She hurried down an aisle toward the fridge units in the back. She pulled open one of the doors and started to pull out the water. The coolness felt great on her over-heated face.

What the fuck was Raider doing here in Hawaii? Of all the times to show up. She hadn't seen him in five years. Not since she'd broken his heart and kicked him to the curb after her world had been turned upside down in a stupid accident on the job. When she'd... when she hadn't told him her reason, to keep his heart from breaking as much as hers had been...

She blinked hard and swallowed convulsively. She couldn't think about that now. She needed to focus on the mission from hell.

She closed the door and started back toward the front of the store. Denlo was talking in a low voice to the guy at the cash register. They both shut up as she approached. What the heck? Did these two know each other? The store attendant was an older guy with short blond hair and mean dark eyes. His long-sleeved shirt gave off weird vibes, especially given how warm it was outside. She could just see the tip of a tattoo on his right arm. His hands had some scars on them like he'd worked construction or some other labor job.

"Got your shit?" Denlo demanded.

She nodded and grabbed the water off the counter, then turned and headed out the door. Raider was standing on the sidewalk just outside of the driveway. He was watching her but making it look like he was drinking water. She gave him another tiny shake of her head. Then she turned the corner and went to the van.

After getting into the driver's seat, she turned and handed out the bottles of water to the guys in the back. She glanced at Vardis, the man the others had carried out. Ashen, sweaty, and not looking in the least healthy. He needed help or he might not make it.

Denlo got into the passenger seat and snarled, "Drive."

She glanced back and watched as Wells and Baker tried to get Vardis to drink some water. He wasn't doing it.

"Drive," Denlo demanded again.

She put the van in gear and pulled out of the parking lot. Heading back towards the hotel seemed like the plan. She wasn't going to ask. Denlo wasn't much of a conversationalist, and he seemed even more terse than usual.

How the hell had she gotten here? Sharing airspace with her ex?

Raider here on the Big Island. Her stomach rolled. He'd seen her. Now he'd be wondering what the hell was going on. *Join the club.*

The weight of Denlo's stare made the side of her face itch. She sent him a sidelong glance.

"You knew that guy in the store," he accused.

Piper's first instinct was to deny it. Tell him she had no idea what he was talking about but she's been so obvious that she didn't think he'd believe her. The last thing she needed was Denlo trusting her even less than he already did. "I..um...we... hooked up a while back. I was just surprised is all."

"What does he know?" Denlo's fingers closed

around the butt of the gun tucked into the front of his belt. *Another damn idiot who'll probably shoot his balls off someday.*

Piper looked in the rearview mirror. Baker and Wells were listening. Vardis was out of it. "He doesn't know much. Like I said we hooked up a while back. There wasn't a lot of talking going on, ya know? I didn't know he was on the island. I thought he was back in San Diego." That was the truth. Or more likely if she allowed herself to think about him at all, she'd think he was in some war-torn country or another.

"Why's he here?"

Piper glanced over to Denlo and shrugged. "I dunno. I didn't talk to him or anything. I was just surprised to see him. I got the water and we left. It's not a big deal. He's just a guy I knew for a couple of weeks like a hundred years ago, okay?" she made her voice sound frustrated and annoyed. *Please let it go.*

"Turn up there," Denlo growled as he pointed to a street on her right.

She made the turn and glanced in the rearview mirror. They weren't being followed. Thanks to the chaos of the evacuation, she doubted anyone had noticed them. The only reason to be thankful for the unexpected volcanic eruption. They could fly under everyone's radars.

Except... Raider had noticed. No doubt about

that. She tried to even out her breathing and stop her stomach from rolling but it was no use. Raider was close by and that was all she was going to be able to think about for a while.

She glanced over at the windows of the homes they were passing. Many were dark. People trying to outrun the lava flow. The volcano was the only thing anyone was talking about. It was all over the news twenty-four-seven. It was why she wasn't so worried about being spotted. But she was worried about what was going on in the back of the van. Vardis's breathing was labored. He sounded like Darth Vader.

She asked in a low voice. "Should we take Vardis to a doctor?" She didn't want to push Denlo, but she had to at least try to get Vardis some help.

Denlo glowered at her but didn't say a word.

Swearing silently, Piper drove on. Sweat broke out on her palms, making her grip slip on the steering wheel. Something bad was about to go down. Being the realist she was, she knew she was powerless to stop it. Denlo was a stone-cold killer. She had no doubts if she asked too many questions, he would have no issue with getting rid of her. They didn't really need a driver for this job.

She glanced in the rearview mirror again only this time she was looking at Vardis. He looked gray in the ambient light coming in as she passed under streetlights. His close-cropped blond hair looked white, making him all together look about seventy instead of in his mid-thirties. His eyes were closed and his breathing was raspy and intermittent, each respiration coming slower and more infrequently. The man's asthma had been made worse as ash accumulated in the air. She knew he'd been using an inhaler, but for the most part, it had been ineffective.

"Turn here," Denlo directed again, and Piper made a right onto a small dirt road that led into the trees. The foliage was thick and scraping on the sides of the van. Finally, they couldn't go any further. Denlo opened his door and got out. He opened the back door and gestured to Baker and Wells.

Wells nudged Vardis but the other man didn't move. Wells had a black mask pulled up over his nose. He was wearing dark jeans, a dark windbreaker, and black sneakers. His hair was black and so were his eyes, but he looked more like a hamster than a killer. His eyes just didn't have the same lethal look that Denlo's had. Wells nudged him again but Vardis didn't move. Baker leaned over and shook Vardis hard, but the other man didn't open his eyes.

"Get him," Denlo directed. The two men dragged Vardis out of the van and the three of them disappeared off into the trees.

"Fuck, fuck, fuck." What the hell was she supposed to do now? She didn't have a cell she could use. Denlo had taken them all. And who the hell would she call? She'd known as soon as she'd stepped onto that plane, there'd be no backup for her. No one was coming to help her. At the time, it had seemed like she'd had no choice, like this was the only path forward if she wanted to get the Snake. Now, she wasn't sure. Maybe she'd finally taken it a step too far.

She stared into the trees. There were few things in life she regretted. She could live with almost all her actions but, one or two events still haunted her. There wasn't much she could do about getting Marta killed. That was on her. But, there was one thing that she could do. She owed Raider an explanation for so much. She owed him the truth about why she threw him out, even knowing his reaction, the loss and devastation he'd feel. The same emotions she had felt. Those memories still haunted her. Seeing him brought it all back. If she got out of this, she'd explain the whole thing and if he hated her well, that was his right. But she would need to get out of this mess first. Unfortunately, the odds of her escape weren't looking so good.

After fifteen interminable minutes, Denlo, Wells, and Baker all climbed back in the van. They weren't dragging Vardis with them. She wanted to ask but decided to keep her stupid mouth shut until she figured out where the hell they were, and also, how the hell she was going to reverse down the sorry excuse for a road they'd driven in on.

An hour later, they were all holed up in a motel on the outskirts of Hilo. Denlo had his own room. Baker and Wells, who seemed to know each other from before. shared a room. She'd shared with Vardis. Now, she was praying Denlo didn't decide to move in. Vardis had been easy to handle. He'd been polite but kept his distance since she'd arrived yesterday. Once the volcano erupted, he'd gone downhill fast.

The shocking bang on her door made her jump. She cursed under her breath and bit her lip. *Get it together. Keep it together.* She took a beat and then opened the door. The three of them were standing outside holding bags from which greasy, fried smells were emanating. Stepping back, she let them into the room and then closed the door after them.

Denlo sat at the table in the corner and the other two joined him. Piper stood back and waited until Baker handed her a burger and some fries. She sat down on the bed. Food wasn't on the list of things she really wanted, but it would look funny if she didn't eat so she took a bite of the burger.

"We have a problem," Denlo said. He wasn't eating. As far as she could tell, they hadn't brought food for him. Odd, yeah, but she wasn't going to question his abstention. Questions would get her killed. Denlo was rail-thin to begin with. Maybe he had stomach issues. His pale blue eyes were in sharp contrast to his bright red skin. He'd been out in the sun at some point before she'd arrived. His close-cropped gray hair made him look like he was in his fifties but then again if he was sick, he could actually be much younger and just didn't look good.

She popped a fry in her mouth and waited.

Denlo continued. "Vardis was our explosives guy. We can't do this job without an explosives expert. We need to find a new one."

Piper stayed silent.

"I know a guy," Baker said as he wiped his greasy fingers on his faded jeans. "He might be available. I've worked with him before."

Baker looked to her to be in his late thirties. He kept his head shaved but wore baggy clothes, barely disguising that he was a mountain of a man with tree trunks for legs. She only knew him as Baker. No one had offered a first name. Slug must have told them her name because they all called her Piper, but no one asked her last name.

Denlo watched Baker eat. "Is he here on the island?"

Baker shook his head. "Nah. He works out of Nashville."

"Won't work then. We need someone here ASAP. Nashville is too far. The boss is trying to locate someone in L.A. We don't have a lot of time. The volcano erupting has moved up the timeline for the job. We go in tomorrow night."

"I don't think that's a good idea," Wells groused. "We need more time to plan. I don't like rushing. You said we had a couple of weeks. Now we're doing it tomorrow night?" He played with the plastic cutlery in front of him.

Denlo glared. "I told you we go when the boss says so. The volcano is a distraction. We don't need as much time to plan because the cops are all busy elsewhere."

"Still," Wells began. "Rushing during a job is always a big fucking mistake. That's how a plan falls apart."

"You better make sure no mistakes happen, or you won't live to complain about it." Denlo fingered the gun at his waist and Wells immediately shut up. He went back to eating his burger.

"Wells has a point," Baker said.

Piper wanted to tell him to shut up. No need to piss Denlo off any further.

"What I mean is," Baker continued cautiously, "we don't have an explosives guy. The plans you gave me don't match the store, which means I can't guarantee where we're gonna come through. And," he pointed at Wells, "he needs time to crack the vault door. He hasn't had enough time to practice. Cracking a safe like that can take hours. It's an all night job and that's if everything goes right."

Denlo leaned forward. "Let me let you in on a little secret. Wells is gonna be able to do it in the time we have. We're doing this now because the volcano erupted and the whole world is busy with that. The risk is lower than if we waited. The boss doesn't give a shit about the details. He just wants it done, so if any of you think you can't do it, now is the time to tell me." He pulled his gun out of his waistband and put it on the table.

No one said a word. Piper glanced down at her food. The little she'd consumed had turned to stone in her stomach. What the fuck had she been thinking of, getting on that plane? She was in way over her head and the chances of finding a way out didn't look good.

Denlo got up, picked up his weapon, and waved it around negligently. "So if you bitches are through with your belly aching then we're done. I'll be in my room. I suggest you do the same. Don't even think about leaving." He gestured with his gun again. "I'll hear it if your room doors open or close. I'm between both rooms. The walls are thin so don't think of trying anything." He waved the gun around one more time and left. They stayed silent. They heard his room door open and then bang closed. The sound of Denlo's voice came through the walls. Piper heard the rumble of Denlo's voice through the wall but couldn't make out the words.

Baker and Wells stared at their food without saying a word. Piper got up and tossed her food into the garbage can. She started back toward the bed when Baker jerked his head at her. He pointed with his chin to the other chair.

Piper swallowed hard as she claimed the seat as directed. She glanced at Wells and then Baker and waited them out.

"I don't fucking like this one bit," Baker whispered.

Wells nodded. "Me either. This isn't the job Slick said it would be. He said it would be professional. This is…a fucking mess."

Hmm. Slug recruited them too. Interesting. She filed away that little tidbit.

"Not much we can do about it," she murmured.

Wells shrugged. "Maybe. Maybe not. If we don't find an explosives expert then the job is off. None of us can blow the floor."

"Then why did you offer your guy?" Piper whispered to Baker.

Baker shrugged. "I was trying to buy us more

time. Because it would take him a while to get here. Besides, it's always better to have someone you know and trust on board."

"What do you think we should do?" Piper asked.

Wells glanced at Baker and leaned forward. "I think we need to stall until it's too late."

Baker shook his head. "I don't know, man. I don't think Denlo is gonna let us stall. If this job goes south, I think he's gonna kill us when the boss says do it, and then start over with a more agreeable crew."

Icy fingers clutched at Piper's heart. She'd been thinking the same thing. If they didn't do this job soon, Denlo would just kill them all and find new people. She decided to take a gamble. "Do either of you know who the boss is?"

They both shook their heads. "Whoever it is, has lots of juice and money," Wells offered. "He got all that equipment no problem and none of it comes cheap."

"You guys have seen it?" Piper was surprised.

Baker nodded. "Yesterday, Denlo took us to a warehouse where the equipment is stored before we picked you up. We've been here longer than you. We're supposed to be working on the plan for the next couple of weeks but when the volcano went, Denlo said everything was moving up and then we went to get you at the airport." He eyed her speculatively.

"Why are you here?" Wells asked straight out.

"Slu...ick said he needed a driver for a job. I said yes and then suddenly I was on a plane." She shrugged. "Not sure why Denlo needs a driver really... but whatever. If I'd known about all this, I never would've gotten on the plane."

"Me either," Baker agreed.

Wells cocked his head and listened. They all did the same. Piper didn't hear anything unusual. The TV in Denlo's room had gone on. It wasn't overly loud but audible enough. He wasn't talking any longer either. Did that mean he would be checking on them?

"I think whoever the boss is, he's here on the island," Wells said conspiratorially. "Denlo was talking to him on the phone when he said that we needed a ladder and some rope. The guy told him to get it at HPM Building Supply. I've never heard of the place. It's local. He told Denlo to ask for Bruce and that the stuff would be ready when he got there."

Baker shrugged. "Could be that the guy just knows the area well. Doesn't mean he's on the island."

"Maybe," Wells conceded, "but it seems like he's here when they talk."

It was food for thought. There was no question that Piper wanted to get the Snake. His presence on the island would make catching his ass easier. But first, she had to survive this job.

"What happened with Vardis?" The words ripped out of her mouth before she could stop herself.

Baker shook his head. "You're better off not knowing."

"Did you…" She left the question open-ended.

Wells looked offended. "His heart was still beating when we left. I ain't that cold-hearted."

Shit, this was bad. They'd left him to suffocate to death. Not a way she'd ever choose to go. "What do you think we should do?" she asked.

Wells glanced at Baker. "I think we do what we're told for now. It's better if we get an explosives guy and then get the job done. If we don't, it's a sure bet Denlo is going to kill us."

Baker shrugged. "I think he's gonna kill us either way. I think we're royally screwed.

4

---

*R*aider stood in the middle of the intersection and pointed at the row of cars ahead of him. He signaled the first pickup to move forward. The driver nodded and entered the intersection. A steady stream of cars followed.

It was going to be a long day. More evacuation zones had been declared overnight, which meant that now thousands of people were trying to get out of harm's way.

A horn blaring to his left captured Raider's attention. A woman was sitting in her convertible pointing at the light. She was the only one trying to cross the intersection from that direction. Raider held up a hand telling her to stay where she was. She was going to have to wait. The line in front of him was long and he needed to get as many people through as he could.

The woman laid on the horn again but he still ignored her. She could wait one more light cycle. Raider watched the cars roll by him. The look of panic and fear on the faces of the drivers hit him in the gut. Most of these people would be fine. The volcano wouldn't end up damaging their property or hurting their family. Likely, this was nothing more than a slight inconvenience and they'd end up with a good story to tell.

For a few, he knew they would be devastated. He'd watched the news last night and hated the insensitive comments to the effect that people built their homes by a volcano, what did they expect? It was logical but not exactly understanding. He knew from experience that people who didn't have much often had to make tough choices. He'd seen it in many places he'd been in the military. Land was cheap on a volcano, like it was in many dangerous areas. People built a home and a life where they could manage it, hoping the threat, in this case a volcano, wouldn't destroy what they'd worked so hard to build.

The steady blare of a car horn pulled him out of his reverie. He gestured for the oncoming traffic to stop and then turned toward the woman. She floored her little black Mercedes convertible and flew across the intersection.

"Asshole," she yelled on her way by.

He shook his head and tried not to laugh

when a moment later he heard the screech of brakes and a loud crunch. Miss Impatient had cut off a truck turning out of the strip mall and he'd smashed the back of her car. Raider turned back to the traffic with a wide grin underneath his black bandana. Karma was a bitch who came for everyone eventually.

Karma had come for him yesterday in the form of Piper Holloway. He fell madly in love the moment he'd seen her across the bar eight years ago. She'd been wearing a pair of ass-hugging faded jeans and a white tank top and she mopped the floor with some guy who'd been hassling her. The guy had hit on her, and she'd told him in no uncertain terms to fuck right off. He'd gotten pissed and grabbed her arm. She'd whirled around and smashed him in the nose. Flattened it across his face. Then, as he bent over and screamed in pain and outrage, she whispered something in his ear. He immediately stopped yelling, grabbed his jacket, and left.

Raider had gone over with a beer and a bag of ice for her hand. "What did you say to that clown?"

She'd tilted her head back and looked up at him a long moment and then said, "Better for you if you never find out."

Then she winked and he was a goner. In that wink, he saw his future. Piper as his wife with three little Pipers running around. After they'd been married for a few months, he'd confessed that if she was okay with it, he'd like to start working on those little Pipers. The whole picture of them with kids looked like heaven to him.

Three glorious years later he'd come home from an overseas tour to find his stuff packed and moved into the hallway. She'd been standing there, arms crossed over her chest. "We're done," she'd said. "I can't take you being gone. It just doesn't work for me."

Raider's heart gave a hard thump as he thought about that day. She refused to say anything else other than, "Don't bother leaving your keys. I had the locks changed." Her delivery, like she was doing nothing more than reading a weather report, had crushed his soul. His happy life just murdered. No Piper, no mini-Pipers running around. No future for them. Nothing. His life had been turned into a wasteland.

The devastating hole he'd crawled into for months was bleak and soul-destroying. It had taken the better part of a year, but Harlan and the rest of the team had finally managed to get him right again. He wouldn't…couldn't…think about her or the family they'd never had. That was the rule. He'd manage as long as he didn't think about all he'd lost. And now she was here on the Big Island. And, because he knew her so well, even after all this time, he was pretty sure she was in trouble.

Two hours later, Raider was in desperate need of water when a van entered the intersection in front of him. It was turning left to go into the strip mall now that the lady with the Merc had been towed away. He glanced at the driver and did a double take. His heart hit his boots. He'd know that blond ponytail anywhere. It didn't matter that she was wearing sunglasses and a surgical-style mask to combat the ashy air. He knew it in his bones that his ex-wife Piper was behind the wheel. And some thug was sitting next to her. The same one from the store last night.

It took everything Raider had not to walk away from his post and follow the van. He watched it out of the corner of his eye. Piper pulled around the back of the strip mall and disappeared. *Not good. None of your business. Do not get involved.* She made it abundantly clear that she was done with Raider when she walked out the door five years ago. "You're never here so what's the difference? I've made a life without you in it. I'm done trying to shoehorn you back in whenever you bother to come home. It's exhausting. Just go, Raider. I'm done. You're just not worth the effort." Those words were branded on his brain, seared into his soul.

The sound of brakes and squealing tires

brought him back to what he was doing. A guy in a pickup had narrowly missed hitting the woman in front of him who'd stopped for a chicken on the road. Raider rushed over and shooed the chicken. The woman smiled her thanks and the man behind shook his head.

Raider returned to the middle of the intersection. He made a futile attempt to focus on traffic, and not watch the strip mall. What the fuck was Piper doing back there with that ruffian? She was working. Why else would she be driving a plain white van behind a strip mall? He studied the surrounding area, but nothing jumped out at him. As he moved a few feet forward to allow a large water truck to make a left, something caught his eye.

And suddenly, Piper's appearance here made sense. In the corner of the strip mall was a bank. It had been hidden from his view by a line of trees. He stared at it. "Fuck," he said aloud as he watched the van pull away from the parking lot and make a right down the street away from him. He knew what she was doing here. She was definitely working. His ex-wife was here to rob a bank.

5

$\mathcal{P}$iper struggled to breathe as she gripped the steering wheel so hard, her knuckles were white. Raider had been at the intersection again. Every time she saw him, emotion hit her like a punch in the gut. Jesus, could it get any worse? What the hell was he doing here? It didn't matter that until last night, she hadn't seen him in five years. As they approached the intersection, she knew instantly it was him directing traffic. She'd know Raider Torres anywhere. He was still just as sexy as the first time she'd laid eyes on him in a bar in San Diego. All lean and tight with the best ass she'd ever seen. His deep brown eyes had gold flecks that sparkled. Her nipples puckered just thinking about him.

"Turn here," Denlo barked.

Piper jumped but cranked the wheel. She'd gotten maybe three hours of sleep when Denlo pounded on her door and said they had to go back out again. Did that mean Raider had been directing traffic all night? Probably. That would be him. Always up for helping out. Always staying until the bitter end whereas she would cut and run as fast as possible.

Denlo growled, "You almost missed the turn. Are you fucking even paying attention?"

She didn't bother to reply to his shouted question but tried to concentrate on her driving, banishing all thoughts of her ex-husband. There would be time enough to think of him when this job was over. She'd lain awake for many nights thinking of him and what she'd done to him, to them. Her callous, abrupt behavior, and worse, his uncomprehending response, would always haunt her.

The silence in the van was tense for the next ten minutes until she pulled into the motel parking lot and parked. Everyone got out of the van.

"Meet in her room," he pointed toward Piper.

Dread filled her. She'd hoped to go into her room and hide. She'd been totally thrown due to how long they'd been inside the store and with Raider right there, she'd felt so exposed. He'd know. He'd know she was working, and he'd start wondering about it.

They took up the same seats they'd had the previous day. Piper leaned against the wall just down from the table. Denlo pulled out his cell and sent off a text.

Baker spoke. "Look, I know you want to do this, Denlo, I mean I know the boss wants to do this, but we can't without an explosives guy. The plans you've given me are all wrong. They don't match up to what I'm seeing. I can't just randomly break down the wall or come through the floor. We've double-checked it now. There's no way. There's no way forward without an explosives guy."

Denlo sat with his arms crossed over his chest. "I don't see why you can't just make a hole in the wall?"

Baker shook his head. "I explained when we were in the store. The walls are reinforced. I don't have the tools to break it down and even if I did, it would be really fucking loud not to mention it would take a long fucking time and the whole building would shake."

"That can't happen," Wells declared. "If the building shakes then the mechanisms on the safe will lock down and there's no way I can open it. It would require a whole system reset and the only people who can do that are bank security. They can't even do it immediately. They have to fly some guy in with codes and some sort of tool to do it. It would take a few days. The door to the safe can't vibrate that much. I told you that before."

Denlo stared at the two men. "If you're making this shit up—"

"No way, man." Wells held up his hands, palms toward Denlo. "I told you this at the beginning. The only way this job goes off is if we have a good explosives expert. He's gotta have a light touch. The floor's gotta blow without shaking the door to the vault."

Denlo's phone went off. He grabbed it off the table and stood up, walking to the other side of the room. "Yeah," he said and then listened. "No, it can't be done. The plans aren't right and they're saying they can't just bust in. It would make the vault door vibrate which would put the whole system on lockdown."

Piper bit her lip. She glanced at Wells and Baker. They looked at her and then each other. She was sure the other two men had the same sinking feeling she did.

Denlo was turned away from them, facing the window. It was early morning, but it wasn't obvious thanks to the falling ash which turned the world gray. Denlo was reflected in the glass. He said something but dropped his voice low so she couldn't make it out. Her body tensed when his hand moved for the butt of the gun stashed in his waistband.

"Yeah, I guess," he said.

She strained to hear more.

"It'll be messy. I'll need help."

Adrenaline rushed through her veins, escalating her heart rate. Denlo was going to kill them all. What the hell? How was she gonna get out of this one?

She bit her bottom lip. There was a way out. One she never thought she'd ever use but it wasn't like she had a choice. Just the thought of it had her breaking out in hives. She didn't want to do it but she wanted to live. Right now, she figured the chances were eighty percent against her survival but if she could work her magic those odds went up to at least fifty-fifty. Still, it was going to be a huge fucking mess and if she did survive, the fall-out would be massive.

Denlo clicked off the call and turned around. He had his gun out of his waistband and down by his side. "We're gonna take a drive," he said and gestured toward the door with the gun.

"I— I might know someone." Piper hated the tremor in her voice. She reined in her galloping heart and spoke again with more confidence. "An explosives expert."

Denlo glared at her. "And you're just coming up with this now?"

"Look, my job is to drive, not supply labor for the gig. I figured you handled that but if it means we're not gonna get paid then I guess I can call a guy."

Denlo came over and aggressively intruded into her personal space. "What guy?"

"The guy from the store yesterday. Like I told you, he's an ex of mine. We've done shit together before. He's an explosives guy. Learned it in the military. He could help us if you give him a decent cut."

Denlo raised his chin. "You said he didn't know anything."

Piper tried to play it cool. She shrugged. "He doesn't… about this job. We haven't seen each other in a while."

Denlo stepped closer to Piper. "Awfully fucking convenient that suddenly you know an explosives guy and you bump into him in the store." He brought his gun up and tapped the barrel on her chest. "Maybe you're a cop. Maybe that's why it's so fucking convenient."

Piper knew this was it. If she didn't convince Denlo, she was a dead woman. She took a step closer to him and yelled, "It's not fucking convenient," she said through clenched teeth. "Not at all. Motherfucker dumped me for some other bitch. I want to cut his heart out with a fucking spoon but we don't got a choice. I didn't fly over here for the fucking good of my health. I wanna get paid. And Slick sent me so you fucking well know I'm not a fucking cop."

Denlo stared at her, keeping the gun leveled at her chest. She refused to look scared or back down. Finally, he lowered the gun. "You trust him?"

"Hell no! But he won't screw up a job." She shrugged. "Up to you but if we can't do the job without an explosives guy then we should give him a call."

Denlo narrowed his eyes at her. "What's his name?"

Piper's mouth was dry as the Sahara and all she wanted to do was guzzle water. Instead, she said, "Rick Sinclair." It had been a cover name that he'd used on some kind of assignment in the past. She had no idea if it would pass any kind of deep dive, but she was guessing Denlo and the Snake didn't have time for a deep dive, so it would probably do. "People call him Raider."

Denlo stared hard at her for a long minute and then he turned and went back to the corner to make a call. He was back in a flash and said, "Make the call," as he handed her the phone. He must have gotten the all-clear from the Snake.

She took the phone. There was no help for it but to dial Raider's cell. If they ran the number they'd discover Sinclair was a false name. Not much she could do about it now. She punched in the digits she'd tried to forget over the last five years.

"Yeah," a familiar voice said over the phone line.

Denlo grabbed her wrist and pulled her arm down, then put the call on speakerphone. Then he gestured toward Piper.

"Hey, Raider, it's Piper." She tried to keep her voice cool but she also needed to warn him not to say anything. "I know it's been a while. Not since that job we pulled up in Silicon Valley. Other than the store yesterday, I mean." She prayed that he would play along.

"Piper," he drawled, "how ya been? I thought that was you. Been a long while." His words were right, but she could hear the slight tension in his voice.

"Not bad, baby. You know how it goes. You?"

"All good, here."

"How are you on the Big Island?" she asked. "The volcano shit is wild."

"Yeah. Crazy. I'm here hanging with friends. Just taking a break."

Denlo glared at her and made a motion with his hand telling her to speed it up.

"Listen, if you're interested, I got a job for you." She did her best to keep her voice level but it was damn hard. Bringing Raider into this mess was a nightmare. They may not be together but she didn't want anything bad to happen to him. Ever.

"What kind of job?" he asked sounding suspicious which is how he should sound if he really were an explosives expert that did illegal shit and a guy who dumped her.

"It's a—"

Denlo ripped the phone out of her hand and turned off the speaker. He put it to his ear. "It's a fucking job that needs a guy that's good with explosives. You in or out?"

Raider must have said something about needing more details because Denlo snarled. "Meet me at the pharmacy." And he gave the address. "Twenty minutes." Then he hung up and gestured to Piper. "You get in the van." He looked at Wells and Baker. "You two stay here in your room. If I find out you went out or you fucked around in anyway, I'll kill both of you. Understand?"

Both men nodded and stood. They all left the room together with Wells and Baker going two doors over and disappearing inside. Piper climbed into the driver's seat of the van and turned it over. Denlo sat in the passenger seat with the gun in his lap. "If this turns to shit, you're the first one to die. I can find any idiot to drive. You get it?"

She bit her lip and nodded. She got it and it scared the hell out of her.

It took her a little more than twenty minutes to get through the traffic to the pharmacy. She pulled into the parking lot and looked for a parking spot. The place was jammed. She found a spot in the far corner and backed in. They sat and waited. She didn't see Raider anywhere but that didn't mean he wasn't there. He was a SEAL, after all.

He used to make a game of sneaking up on her. No matter how she tried to be prepared, he still managed to get her. It was frustrating as hell but also endearing and it was one of the things she missed most about him. She missed a lot of things about him. Almost everything, as a matter of fact. She swallowed hard. Now wasn't the time to think about all that ancient history. She cleared her throat and looked around the parking lot.

"Your friend is late. He doesn't show in the next five minutes and we're out of here." Denlo jostled the gun in his lap.

Piper glanced around the parking lot once more. "There," she said breathing a sigh of relief. Raider was making his way across the parking lot towards them. Denlo got out of the van and Piper followed suit. They met in the front.

"Piper," Raider said as he leaned down and gave her a big hug. "Good to see ya, girl."

Piper wanted to respond but suddenly her

throat closed over with tears and she couldn't get any words out. The hug was brief but damn if it didn't feel good. Really good.

"She says you're good with explosives," Denlo growled.

Raider nodded. "Yeah, I am."

He looked good. Tanned and fit. Maybe even more relaxed than usual. His eyes weren't constantly scanning the parking lot. Oh, she didn't doubt that he knew exactly where everyone was and which cars were more likely to have a gun in the glove box but he didn't have the slightly haunted look he used to have. Maybe divorce agreed with him. That thought was like a sucker punch to the gut.

She'd missed some of their conversation and cursed herself for getting caught up in seeing Raider. Denlo seemed to be pissed about something. "I need to know if you've got any experience. Just cuz she says you're good doesn't mean you are. I need someone with a subtle touch."

"I'm a demolitions expert with military training. I can be delicate. I can blow the pimple off the ass of a donkey. What do you need done?"

Denlo shook his head. "Uh-uh. First I need to check you out. Give me some references."

Raider shook his head. "You know my name. You look me up. Get back to me tomorrow."

"No. I'll look you up, Sinclair, but it will be in

53

a couple of hours. If it's a go, she'll call you and you'll come meet us. I tell you the job then."

"What do I get paid?" Raider demanded. "I'm not agreeing to do a job without knowing how much I get paid."

Denlo nodded. "You pass the test and I'll tell you all the details you want." He gestured to Piper to get back in the van. "Keep your phone on."

Piper got behind the wheel and made eye contact with Raider. He gave her a slight, fast nod, one she was pretty sure Denlo missed because he was busy adjusting the gun in the front of his pants. Raider turned and strolled back across the parking lot like he didn't have a care in the world, or that a volcano was in the process of blowing its top. And yes, he still had the best ass she'd ever seen. Now she just had to hope she hadn't involved him in something that was going to get it shot off.

6

"*D*ude, stay away. You know it's not gonna end well," Harlan commented.

"It didn't the first time round and now she's draggin' you into some shit. I'm just tellin' ya it won't go well."

Raider gripped the phone. His buddy was not wrong. He hadn't seen Piper in five long years, and recovering from the soul-crushing agony when she'd kicked him out hadn't been pretty.

"She's in trouble." Raider knew it as sure as he was standing in the deli. Piper was in serious trouble. He'd looked around when he met her in the parking lot and when she had been behind the strip mall. She had no backup. If someone had been there for her, he'd have spotted them. He was trained to spot all kinds of things and baby girl was flying solo. His gut tightened.

"All the more reason to just stay the hell away. Brother, it took you a long time to get over her. I'm still not sure you're there. Look at your dating history. You never date anyone longer than a few months. Getting involved with Piper isn't gonna make things better."

The guy behind the counter yelled out his name and Raider stepped up to grab his sandwich. There weren't many people left on this side of the island, but they all seemed to be in that little shop. Misery likes company and these people all needed to commiserate. Of course, it was one of the few shops still open and providing service. The only other place he'd noted that was open for business seemed to be the convenience store. At least on this stretch of road.

"I hear what you're saying but I can't leave her out there on her own." He walked out of the store and slid behind the wheel of his borrowed pickup.

"What happened to her people? Shouldn't they be with her? Can't she ask them for help?"

All legit questions and he'd had the same ones. "I guess not. It's weird. I hear what you're saying and you're right. I know you're right."

"But…" Harlan sighed, "You're not gonna listen to me are you?"

"No."

"Dammit, Raider. You never listen with the right head."

"This isn't about that," he retorted.

"Yeah. Sorry.' Harlan's tone conveyed his remorse far better than his words. "Listen, keep me in the loop. I'll fill the others in. You need us, you call."

"Will do. I gotta go. Thanks, buddy." He clicked off the call and answered the incoming one. "Hey, Hawk, thanks for getting back to me." He was relieved to hear Jace Hawkins voice.

"No worries. What's up?"

Raider hated to ask but he figured he would make it up to the guy somehow. "I need a favor."

"Shoot."

"I think a friend of mine is in trouble. It's kind of a long story but my guess is she needs some help. I've heard a lot of good things about you and the Brotherhood Protectors, and I was wondering if you can backstop a cover for me quick time."

There was a beat of silence and then. "Sure. What's the name?"

"Rick Sinclair. I need to be an explosives expert. Military trained. You can use my real background for the rest of it. You can look me up."

"Okay. I'll have something up shortly. Fair warning… It won't hold up if they dig too much but if they give it a cursory glance then it should be fine." Hawk paused then asked, "Is there any point in asking what's going on?"

"To be honest, I'm not sure just yet. I… I just need to make sure my friend is okay." He didn't want to lie to Hawk but he wasn't up to getting into the details. "Talk to Harlan if you need some more background. He can fill you in."

"Okay. We'll have you up and running in thirty."

"Man, I can't thank you enough for this."

"No worries. You guys are helping us out. This is nothing. A few keystrokes. You let me know if you need anything else."

"Thanks, buddy." Raider hung up. The knots in his stomach eased ever so slightly. Now he just had to hope that whoever was running the check was lazy or they were desperate. Either way worked for him.

Two hours later his phone rang again. "'Lo?"

"Raider," Piper's voice came through the phone. "Meet us back at the pharmacy parking lot." She disconnected the call.

It was hard to tell with that short exchange, but he was pretty sure she was scared. Whatever was going on had her rattled. He glanced at the seat beside him. He'd bought a few burner cells and a few other things. Never hurts to be prepared. He tucked one cell in his boot and the other in the leg pocket of his black cargo pants.

Chances were good, he'd lose the one in his pocket. The thug with Piper looked like the controlling type, but with any luck, he'd hopefully keep the one in the boot. He added a short-bladed dagger to his other boot and then got out of the truck. He walked across the parking lot.

The same guy from earlier got out of the van but Piper stayed behind the wheel. She'd kept her sunglasses on but she was biting her lip. He'd always hated when she did that because it meant she had doubts. Or afraid. Neither was ever a good sign.

"Get in," the man said.

"No." Raider wasn't stupid. Once he got in the van all negotiation was over and chances were good he'd be stuck in whatever mess Piper was involved in. He wanted to at least get a feel for it first.

"Get in the fucking van," the man growled.

"Do I look like a fuckin' idiot to you?" Raider countered. "You tell me what the job is and what you need me to do in detail. If my gut doesn't tell me I'm fucked, then we'll talk about transportation. And I need to know if you've got the right equipment. Also, I want to know what I'll be paid."

The man glared at him, his jaw working. He squinted around the parking lot but it was much emptier than it had been earlier. People were leav-

59

ing. The air was thick with ash. Raider had taken his bandana off to eat and regretted not putting it back on. The volcano wasn't letting up and it wasn't looking good. Houses had already been lost to the lava flow.

"I need you to blow a hole in a floor. We're coming up from underneath. You need to do it as quietly as possible, not too much noise or vibration in the floor. There's something that could... break if it rattles. You've got about fifty feet between the hole and the target that needs to stay solid. Think you can do it?"

Raider ran quickly through his options as he stared at the thug. They were for sure robbing the bank. If the vault door felt too much vibration it would automatically go into lockdown mode and they'd need something special to unlock it.

Raider cocked his head. "Depends. What's the floor made of?"

The guy looked at him and shrugged. "Fuck if I know. What are floors usually made of? I got a guy who can answer those questions. So you in?"

He still hesitated. His gut was telling him this was bad news. The whole thing was screaming at him to run in the opposite direction but then he glanced at Piper, still sitting stone-faced behind the wheel. *Shit*. "How much?"

The man looked at him. "Fifty K."

Raider shook his head. "Nope. You're doing

something big and this is last minute which means you lost your original guy. A hundred K."

The guy grunted. "Double? No fucking way."

"No deal then. See ya." Raider turned to go.

"Fine, fucking one hundred thousand but you better be fucking amazing at this or I'll kill you myself."

Raider turned back, his stomach doing a flip-flop. The speed this guy agreed to doubling the amount was bad news. "Fine."

"Get in the fucking van."

Raider shrugged. "I need to grab some clothes. I'll meet you—"

"Get in the fucking van. We're doing this tonight. You don't need clothes."

Another bad sign. "Okay," he started toward the van. "What do I call you?"

"Denlo."

Raider climbed into the vehicle's cargo space. The van rocked as Denlo hoisted himself into the front passenger seat. Piper put it in gear and they rolled out of the parking lot. The entire drive was spent in silence. They didn't go far, only about three miles but it took a while. The roads were still lousy with people leaving and more and more avenues of retreat were being closed off because of the lava flow.

Piper pulled into the parking lot of a no-tell motel and parked outside of a room on the back side of the sleazy place. She and Denlo got out. Raider followed suit.

"Follow her," Denlo growled. Raider said nothing as he followed Piper into a room. Two other men came out of a room two doors down and joined them. Piper closed the door and took a seat on the bed. The two men sat in the chairs at a small table.

Denlo turned to Raider and said, "Put your hands on the wall."

"What?"

"On the wall," Denlo demanded.

Raider turned and did what he was told but swore as Denlo body searched him. "Take it easy, buddy. I'm not carrying."

Denlo pulled out the cell from his pocket but didn't bother with the boots. Raider made a mental note; Denlo hadn't been formally trained. In some ways that was good, but it also meant that he might do something really fucking dumbass at the wrong moment. Always a happy thought.

Denlo plopped down at the table. Raider turned and leaned on the wall. "So tell me details. What's the set up?"

Denlo nodded so the one called Baker started talking. "We're going in through the floor of the bank. There's an empty store beside it. They used to be one space so the storage beneath the store extends under the bank. We want to come up through the floor close to the front. The vault is in the back corner."

Raider nodded. "What's the floor made out of?"

"The usual. Concrete and then a subfloor and then padding and carpet."

"You sure it's not reinforced?" Raider asked. It would be really unusual for the floor of a bank not to be reinforced with steel.

"It's not," Denlo supplied. "We know the guy who redid the space when the bank moved in. He did the walls but not the floor. Deemed too expensive. It's just a small local bank."

Raider nodded but he was trying to sort through what he'd just heard. Why the hell would they rip off a small local bank in a strip mall? There wouldn't be much money in that. Not with it being closed from the volcano.

He refocused and dropped into the role of an explosives specialist. "What kind of equipment do you have?"

Denlo gave him the rundown. C4 and blasting caps with all the wiring he'd need.

Raider asked, "Where are the plans?"

Baker looked at Denlo but didn't say anything.

Raider's shoulders tightened. "You have plans, right? Blueprints? You've gotta have blueprints for a job like this."

Baker cleared his throat. "Ah, the blueprints we have don't seem to match what's going on."

"What?" Raider's stomach dropped. "You can't pull a job like this if you don't have the right blueprints. Jesus, what is this? Amateur hour?" He glared at Piper. "What the fuck did you get me into, girl?" He had to play it right. If he didn't Denlo would get suspicious. Piper didn't meet his gaze. Another bad sign. This whole thing was a cluster fuck and he'd let her drag him into it.

Denlo pulled his gun out. "You need to fucking calm down. You said you can do the job so you're gonna do the job."

Raider looked at Baker and Wells. They were both staring at the table. *What a shit show*. "How do you know the blueprints don't match up?" Maybe he could figure something out."

"I've tried checking the walls but things aren't where they should be. The power isn't where it should be and neither is the plumbing. I should be able to detect the piping and the wiring when I run a Walabot over the walls and it's not there."

The advanced tool for seeing what was behind walls was great, but not nearly as good as some of the military's top-secret tech. Raider grunted. "Let me see."

Everyone remained silent as Baker left the room. He was back in under a minute with a messily folded set of blueprints. He laid them out on the bed. Raider leaned over to study them. "Show me what you're talking about."

Baker pointed out the shared wall with the store and talked about what he should be able to find there. "But none of it is there."

Raider studied the plans. "Has anyone been inside? Do we know for sure that the vault is in the back corner?"

"Yes," Denlo nodded, "I've been in and it's in the back corner. The tellers are in front and there are offices off to the side."

"But you can't see this wall from the front of the bank, right?" Raider asked as he tapped a line on the prints.

Denlo conceded that it was blocked by the offices.

"Well, fuck me. We really don't know what the hell is going on. Shit." He stared at the blueprints some more.

"Can't you just blow a hole here in the front and we can go up?" Denlo demanded.

Raider stared at him. "I can blow a hole here in the front," he pointed to the plans but then you're gonna be too close to the front window and even a small blast could shatter it. We need to come up behind the line of teller stations but over to this side." He turned to Baker. "Let me see the basement blueprints."

Baker put those on the other bed. Raider

scanned them for a minute, then turned and looked at the bank's blueprints once more. "We've got a serious problem."

"No, we don't," Denlo growled as he stood up. "You need to blow a hole and make this fucking work."

Raider straightened. "I can blow a hole but the storage space isn't deep enough to do it where we'd be in the clear which means in order for me to blow the hole and not break the front window or make the vault door vibrate too much, I have to blow a hole here." He pointed to an office space.

Baker bent over and looked at both sets of blueprints. "Shit, he's right. The storage space isn't deep enough. He's gotta blow it in the office." Baker blanched as he said the words.

"So blow it in the office. What's the big deal?" Denlo argued.

"You ever been in a bank office?" Raider asked. "They're fucking tiny usually. If I blow a hole in this one and there're chairs or a desk or a filing cabinet above, it's gonna come crashing down on top of us and make a hell of a noise."

"He's right," Wells agreed. "It could also set off the vault door if it was a big enough piece of furniture."

Denlo glowered. "I don't give a shit what you have to do but you're gonna get us into that bank tonight." He gestured with his gun. "You two, back to your room." Baker and Wells looked at each other and Baker gave a little shrug. They headed out the door.

Denlo turned to Piper. "He's in here with you. If he does anything stupid or tries to leave, it's on you and I'll kill him and you. Understand?"

Piper nodded and Denlo went out the door. She turned and held up her hand to Raider to stop him from saying anything. She cocked her head. Raider listened. Denlo entered his room and turned the TV on and then it sounded like he was making a phone call because Raider could hear him talking but couldn't hear what he was saying.

Piper sat down at the table. "I'm sorry for dragging you into this, Raider, but I didn't have a choice." She kept her voice low and barely glanced at him.

Raider remained anchored in the middle of the room between the double beds. "How come you didn't have a choice? What happened to the original explosives guy? And where the hell is your backup? I didn't see any in the pharmacy parking lot. They may be ATF but I can usually spot them a mile away."

Piper refused to hold his gaze. Raider's chest knotted. "You don't have backup, do you?"

She shook her head once.

Raider swore. "Does your boss at the ATF even know you're here?"

"I told him before I got on the plane but there was no time for him to do anything. I've only been here a day. I'm assuming he's putting things in place but…" she shrugged.

"You've got no idea and no way to check." Raider wanted to put his fist through the wall. This whole op was impulsive and reckless, not like the Piper he knew. She was a great agent. Solid, knew when to push and when to back off. Yeah, she might have pushed a little hard sometimes, but she had never been one to risk her life. He stared at her.

It would be so easy to yell at her, tell her how stupid this all was, that their lives were in danger because of her stupidity and her ego. But he held back. Being out of control now wasn't gonna help either of them. In his gut, he knew there had to be more to the story, a lot more.

He crossed his arms over his chest and took a steadying breath. "Why did you get on the plane?" There had to be a reason. Piper might be impulsive, but he could not recall a time when she'd been totally reckless. There was always a method to her madness.

"The Snake."

"What?" Raider asked completely confused.

"The guy who's running this job. I call him the

Snake," she said with a sigh. "He has a Snake tattoo on his arm. I've never seen his face, but I've seen the tattoo."

Raider frowned. This was personal for her. "Out with it, Piper."

She bit her lip and swallowed. "My unit was on a stake-out, watching this warehouse. We knew guns were coming in, a big shipment and we knew that the son of a bitch running the op was going to be there to oversee the deal. There had been some issues and he wanted to reassure the buyers that everything would run smoothly. At least that's what our guy on the inside said. He was one of the buyers. He'd raised a fuss since the last deal had gone south so the Snake was going to be there, and we were finally going to be able to put a face on this guy."

She glanced down at the table and then back at Raider. "They were late. Our guy was there with the buyer but no guns and no shot caller. It didn't help that Assistant Director Fielding was there. I have no idea why he thought it was a good idea for him to be in on the raid but there was not much anyone could do about it. Added pressure on everyone you know? Anyway, the buyers were thinking of leaving when a van arrived. They drove directly into the warehouse, and we lost visual."

She stopped talking again and Raider's

stomach sank to his knees. He knew what was coming. "My partner, Marta, and I infiltrated the warehouse to try to get a visual. We were hiding behind some pallets and trying to establish a line of sight when shots were fired. I went left to another set of pallets and peeked around. The van's back door was open and the shooter was hunkered down with an assault weapon. The buyers and our guy didn't stand a chance.

"The van door closed, and they started out. I stood up and fired until I was empty. Marta did the same thing except someone started shooting back from somewhere inside the warehouse. I took cover behind the pallets again and made my way towards Marta. I was about twenty feet away when I saw her. She was crouched down behind a stack of lumber. This guy came out of nowhere. He was wearing a jacket with a hoodie underneath like the dockworkers do and he had the hood up. He stood in front of Marta and said, 'Tell your people to stop harassing me or I'm gonna kill you all one by one.' Then he shot her in the stomach. The sleeve of his jacket rode up a couple of inches and I saw the snake tattoo."

She swallowed hard again. "There was nothing I could do since I was out of ammo so I just held Marta until help arrived. They were there so fast, but not fast enough. She died in my arms." Piper finally met Raider's gaze straight on.

"I want him, Raider. I want his fucking head on a platter. He killed Marta. He needs to go down."

Raider cursed up a storm in his head. This had been a fool's errand from the beginning. Remembered hurt and pain were etched in his ex-wife's face and her expression made his chest tighten even more. He moved involuntarily, like he wanted to go over and hug her. Tell her it was all going to be okay. That they'd get this Snake and that would make it all better, but the truth was, it wouldn't.

He stayed put between the beds. "Nothing will bring Marta back and you getting yourself killed won't fix it either. I know you know this so why did you get on the plane?"

"It's my fault Marta is dead. I said we should try and get a visual on the inside of the warehouse. If we'd stayed outside, Marta would still be alive."

And there it was. The real reason Piper got on the airplane. It was still unlike her though. He couldn't shake his belief that there was still a missing piece of the puzzle. Why did she push to go into the warehouse in the first place? "You don't know that," he said finally. "Did Marta fight you on going in?"

Piper shook her head. "No, she was game. Marta was always up for anything."

"Then she knew what she was getting into and

the only one responsible for her death was the guy who shot her." A thought hit him and he froze. "You're not on suspension, are you?" Jesus, did the ATF decide she was responsible? They'd investigate for sure in that situation.

"No. They said what we'd done was within the parameters of the op. There was no way we could've known there was a shooter inside the warehouse. We had it under surveillance and somehow he got by us. They're still investigating that part."

Piper ran a hand over her face and Raider instantly felt his groin tighten. He'd always been a sucker for a woman in trouble, but Piper was another class all together. She was so strong in her own right that when she showed vulnerability it was like someone turned up the wattage on his protective instincts by a thousand percent. She was still his kryptonite. He still wanted her so badly his balls ached.

"Alright. Okay. What happened to the other explosives guy," Raider instructed as he quietly searched the drawers.

"Vardis. That's the only name I knew him by. He apparently had asthma. The ash seemed to trigger some kind of attack that his inhaler couldn't control. His breathing got really labored. Last night when we were leaving the store and I bumped into you, Vardis was in the van semiconscious. When we left, Denlo made me drive into the rainforest area until I couldn't go any further and then he and Wells and Baker carried Vardis into the woods. I have no idea what they did with him. They came back maybe fifteen minutes later without him, and we left."

Raider nodded. "Do you know where you were?"

Piper hesitated. "Sort of? I can guess an area. If I had a map, I might be able to find it or at least narrow it down but at this point..." she shrugged.

Raider bent down and pulled a cell out of his boot.

"Seriously? You might have mentioned that," Piper chided.

He ignored her comment as he walked over and turned on the TV. Then he powered up the cell and strode into the bathroom. The window was on the small side and they might have been able to get out except some asswipe had nailed it shut. Opening it would make a lot of noise which would alert Denlo. He put the option on the back burner. He'd found nothing else in the room that would be useful but at least he had the knife in his boot.

He punched in a number. "Kian," Raider said softly as the other man answered.

"Dude, I heard you ran into your ex. Tough

break and just when I was starting to like the Big Island," his friend commented.

"Yeah," Raider said as he ran a hand through his hair. "Listen, I need you to do something. There's a guy in the rainforest and he needs medical help. I'm not even sure he's alive but you gotta go find him."

"Shit man, what the hell does Piper have you mixed up in?"

"It's a long story and I can't talk much."

Kian whistled. "That bad? Do you need us to pull you out?"

Raider stared at Piper. He wanted her to get out, to be safe but he knew if he blew this op now she'd just go put herself into some other wild situation that would be just as bad or worse, and he might not be there to help her. He gritted his teeth. "Not just yet."

"Raider, man, are you sure? Your head's not so good around that woman. Me and Waylen can come save your ass like we always do."

"Funny." Raider shook his head. Even now Kian was giving him a hard time. "I just need you to find the guy."

"Seriously," Kian said, "if you need help or whatnot, just say the word. I don't like that she's got you mixed up on something we don't know shit about."

"Thanks, I'll reach out if I need you."

"Fine. Where the hell am I going? And what was wrong with this guy?" Kian asked.

"Asthma that the ash set off."

Kian grunted. "Lot of that going around."

"Here's Piper. She's gonna tell you where she thinks the guy is."

Piper took the phone and immediately launched into the description of the route she took. When she finished, Kian must have asked some questions because she repeated some things and tried to add more detail. Then there was a long silence at which point her face flushed and then lost all its color. She handed the phone back to Raider and went into the bathroom, closing the door behind her.

"What did you say to her?" Raider demanded.

"Shit that needed saying. I've got this. I'll see if I can find the guy. You call if you need help. If none of us hear from you in twenty-four hours, we're coming for you."

"Deal." Raider hung up.

He handed the phone to Piper. "Call your people. If we're gonna break into a bank, I'd like to not go to jail."

Piper reluctantly took the phone and then went into the bathroom. She turned on the shower and closed the door.

Raider shook his head. Twenty-four hours and this should all be over...if Denlo didn't decide to kill them all first. This job gave him all kinds of the willies. The whole thing didn't quite add up. Twenty-four hours and he'd be back to enjoying retirement. Or he'd be six feet under. Neither choice appealed to him but bored was a hell of a lot better than dead.

7

*P*iper tried to gather herself. Kian had told her that if she hurt Raider again she'd have to answer to him. She didn't blame him. What she'd done to Raider was unforgivable. If they all knew the truth, they would never even speak to her. Raider certainly wouldn't be here helping her now.

She leaned against the sink and tried to push all the pain and sadness and grief back down deep in her soul. *What's done is done.* There was no fixing it. She'd had to move on and she'd known she couldn't do that if she saw Raider every day. The loss hurt her, but she'd never get over the hurt she'd caused him. Had she spared him by not telling him the facts behind her reasons? At the time, she thought she had. Didn't matter how often she told herself she'd done the right thing, the truth still hurt so damn much. She couldn't bear to think he'd have been in as much pain as she was. But in the end, aren't the people you love supposed to help you through this kind of thing? She hadn't helped Raider, and by not telling the truth, she'd denied him the opportunity to help her.

She dialed her boss. "Chambers," his voice came down the line.

"It's me."

"Where are you?" he demanded.

"At a small motel just outside of Hilo. Are you here on the Big Island?"

"Yes, but we're around the other side. We're trying to get set up with the locals but with the volcano, no one has time for us. We don't have any resources. We're kind of screwed here. What the hell were you thinking getting on that plane?" His voice was harsh and full of the anxiety that she felt down to her toes.

"I...I was thinking it's our chance to get the guy in charge, the one who killed Marta. I—"

"The only thing you're gonna get is yourself killed," Chambers cut her off. "We've got nothing here. Locals are all caught up in the volcano shit and the ATF office on Oahu is involved in some big bust. They might be able to swing some help but they're not sure." John Chambers swore again.

"Jesus, Piper, the higher-ups are all over me on this. Even if we get you out of this, I'm not sure you'll have a job left to come back to."

That was a punch to the solar plexus. All the air left her lungs. No job…what the hell had she been thinking? What were they supposed to do? She disobeyed a direct order. "I…I get it. I'll… worry about that later. In the meantime, this is what's going on." Piper spent the next few minutes filling her boss in. "Look, I gotta go. I'm not sure if I'll get a chance to call again but I'll do my best to reach out."

"Piper…just be careful."

She let out a half laugh. *Too late for that.* She hung up and stared at herself in the mirror for a second. No question she'd really screwed up this time. She came out of the bathroom and sat down at the table facing the door. She needed to keep physical distance from Raider, or she just might throw herself into his arms. It was the only place she'd ever felt truly safe.

Raider closed a drawer and stood facing her. "Nothing here we can use as a weapon."

"No," she agreed. "I already looked."

She held the phone out to Raider. He grabbed it as the room door opened with no warning. Raider immediately palmed the phone. Piper stood and the two turned towards the doorway. Denlo stood there his hand on his gun. "We've got to move. They just declared this an evacuation zone. Cops are going to be coming around. We need to be out of here ASAP."

Raider grabbed the blueprints off the bed and rolled them up. Piper followed him and Denlo out of the room to the van. She got behind the wheel and they pulled out of the lot.

"Where to?"

Denlo was on his cell but whoever he was calling wasn't answering. "Fuck. I don't know. We need to be close. Let me think."

"Are there other motels?" Baker asked.

"Yes, moron but they're all in the zone. We'd have to go well outside of Hilo to be outside of the zone and now they're saying the lava might cut off the highway. We need to stay close."

Piper glanced in the mirror and met Raider's gaze. The pure clusterfuck factor was getting worse by the minute. She regretted pulling him into this. She should've toughed it out on her own. If anything happened to him—It didn't bear thinking about. She tried to apologize to him with her eyes. She wasn't sure she'd be able to get the words out later.

Raider broke off the eye contact. "We could go stay in one of the developments that are in the earlier evacuation zones. Those houses are all empty. No one will be looking there. The cops have already swept through. They won't be going back. Everyone who would leave has already gone. As long as we avoid anyone who stayed we should be fine."

Denlo glanced back at Raider for a minute but then nodded. "Yeah. That works." He glanced at his phone screen and started giving directions. Twenty minutes later they were driving through a deserted neighborhood. The houses all looked abandoned. They did pass one that had a dog outside on the front porch but that was the only sign of life.

Denlo directed her to go further up the hill. "Stop," he said a few minutes later. They were at the mouth of a road. It was narrow but there was a mailbox so she assumed it was a driveway, but she couldn't see the house. "Turn here." He indicated the driveway.

She made the right turn and started up. The driveway curved to the right and then the house appeared. It was a ranch-style house, all on one level but it was large. Tropical plants and flowers in neat beds added a riot of colors. The house had large windows and was painted a soft gray with white trim. A two-car attached garage was on the right side of the house.

"Stop here." Denlo got out and went to the front door. He rang the bell and waited. No one answered. He knocked but again no one answered. He rattled the knob but the big red door was locked. He looked in the side windows. Suddenly, he pulled out his gun and used the butt to break the glass. He made a hole large enough to put his hand through and a second later he opened the door, then disappeared inside.

Piper fought the urge to throw the van in reverse and get the hell out of there. She reached for the gear shift when the garage door suddenly started up. Denlo must have realized his mistake because he was squatting down with the gun pointed directly at her. So much for that plan. She should've been faster.

She pulled the van into the garage, and they all piled out as the garage door rolled closed. They trooped into the house through a mud room and into the kitchen. It was weird breaking into someone's home. Piper sent up a mental note of apology and then walked from the kitchen into the great room area.

A massive pool took up a good amount of space in the backyard, along with a barbeque area. Neat and tidy landscaping was pleasing to look at, and it was clear whoever lived here was house proud. They also had money. White cabinets, light wood floors, and white stone countertops created a designer look in the kitchen. The appliances were stainless steel. There was even a TV on the wall opposite the great room so someone could watch it while making dinner.

She walked back in and opened the fridge. Whoever lived here had left in a hurry because the fridge was fully stocked. Her stomach rumbled.

"You"—Denlo said as he came from a hallway across the great room, pointing the gun at Raider —"come with me." He swung the gun toward Piper. "You too."

Piper glanced at Raider but did as she was told. Her heart slammed against her ribcage and she shoved her hands in her pockets to hide the tremor. They went down a hallway into a large bedroom. It had to be the primary one for the house. The floor was covered by a cream carpet and the bed had a cream duvet with lots of accent pillows in reds and yellows and blues. A bathroom was off to the left and a set of sliding glass doors led to a deck on the right.

"In here," Denlo said. He pointed towards the closet.

Piper glanced at him as she went by but he just glared at her. The walk-in closet was huge by closet standards, with clothes all along the perimeter and a large island in the middle with a stone surface that matched the kitchen's. There were some clothes on it along with a towel. No windows in the walls to provide light, just a skylight above the island. She turned towards Denlo. "What the hell is going on?"

Raider was standing in the closet off to her left.

"Me, Baker, and Wells are going to get the equipment for tonight. You two are going to stay here. I'm locking you in. Don't do anything stupid." With that, Denlo closed the door and then there were muffled sounds from outside. She went over and tried the knob. It turned but she couldn't budge the door.

"It's not a regular closet." Raider was leaning against the only bit of exposed wall.

"What do you mean?" Piper put her shoulder to the door and shoved again, but all she got for her effort was a sharp stinging pain.

"I think this is a redo of something else. Maybe it was a garage bay at one point, I don't know but the floor is concrete, and the door opens out. He's got us trapped. I assume he moved some kind of furniture or something in front of the door. We're in here for the duration."

Piper stifled the scream surging up her throat. The closet might be big by closet standards, but she did not want to be in there with Raider. "Shit. Is there any way out?"

Raider shook his head. He slid down the wall until he was sitting on the floor with his legs stretched out in front of him. He crossed them at the ankles. "Might as well get comfortable. We'll be here a while. Good time to get some sleep." He closed his eyes and tilted his head back against the wall.

Piper stared at him. She couldn't decide if she wanted to strangle him or jump his bones. Heat bloomed in her lady parts answering that question, so she looked up at the skylight. It wasn't that high. Shoving an old towel aside, she climbed up onto the island and stood up. The skylight was on an angle so she could actually see out. "Holy shit!"

Raider was on his feet in an instant. "What is it?" he asked as he scrambled up beside her.

They both stared out of the skylight at the glowing river of lava. It was flowing down the mountain in the distance. It wasn't coming towards them but running on a parallel route. "Raider, this is crazy."

"Yeah," he agreed. "We should get out of here. The hell with the bank job and catching Snake."

He turned toward her. She blinked. She wanted to agree but…Marta's death still haunted her. She bit her lip. This was as close to the Snake as she'd ever come.

"Forget I said that." Raider jumped down. "But I'm telling you right now, if the lava gets closer, we're out of here, Snake or no Snake." He settled back down on the carpet.

Piper stared out the skylight. He was right. This was stupid. She was risking both their lives and there was no guarantee she was going to meet the Snake. She bit back a sigh and started to hop off the island. She slipped on the towel and went sailing off backward. Arms clamped around her and the two of them hit the closet floor, Piper on top of Raider.

"*Oof.*" Raider made a sound as they landed.

Piper took a second to gather herself. She was plastered down the length of her ex-husband and it felt glorious. She lifted her head. "Are you okay?"

He opened one eye and met her gaze. "You've lost weight."

She rolled her eyes. It was time to get up or she might do something that she'd regret. Or that he'd regret. She pushed against him to get up when he suddenly flipped her over so she was on the bottom and he was on top, nestled between her thighs. She stared up at him, mouth open in surprise.

"Why?" His gaze bored into hers.

She knew what he was asking but it was too much, too hard to answer. "I can't, Raider. Just let it go."

He didn't budge. "You never once told me the truth. Why? It's not like we had kids or even a dog but I was still your husband and I deserve to know."

She swallowed convulsively as panic gripped

her throat. Could she tell him the truth? She desperately wanted, to share the burden but she knew in her heart of hearts he'd never forgive her. It was better that he hated her for kicking him out than hated her for what she'd done. This way he'd get over it. If she told him the truth, she was afraid he never would. She wouldn't.

"Raider, please let it go," she pushed against his chest.

"No. I deserve the truth." He shifted so he covered her entire body with his. He put an elbow on either side of her head. "I'm not letting you up until you tell me."

She closed her eyes. This wasn't the way she wanted to say it. Not here. Not like this. She didn't want him to find out like this. "Raider, this isn't the time."

"Like hell. It's as good a time as any."

She knew by the set of his jaw that he wasn't going to give up but there was no way she could fight him. The weight of him on top of her made her nipples harden. She could tell him but he'd be so angry, so devastated that he'd lose focus and then their lives would be in even more danger. At least that was her excuse. His face so close to hers, there was no choice, no choice at all. She lifted her head and kissed him. Put her lips on his and then opened her mouth.

Raider didn't hesitate. He kissed her back, his

tongue doing a familiar dance with hers. God, she'd missed this. Their connection…the man. Piper wound her hands around his back and arched her hips into his. He lowered her head to the carpet and deepened the kiss. Piper reveled in it. There had been times she'd thought she'd die from missing his touch, his kiss, his everything. Every emotion she'd crammed away surged through her.

She moved her legs out from under his and wrapped them around his legs as she arched higher against him. He ran his hand down her side until he found the edge of her t-shirt then he pulled it up. She gasped when his hand landed on her breast and then pushing her bra aside, he tweaked her nipple. She let out a groan.

Running her hands down over his ass, she pulled him closer as she rubbed against his growing hard-on. She wanted this so badly. Not a night went by when she didn't dream of it. There hadn't been any other man in the five years since she'd kicked him out. She just couldn't bring herself to let another man touch her. She was Raider's. Always had been his no matter what she's said or done.

Piper was reaching for his belt when there was a sound at the door. Raider was up on his feet in seconds. She was slower but managed to get up and sorted by the time the door opened. Denlo stared at the two of them. His eyes narrowed but he didn't say anything. He stepped back, hand still on the damn gun. "We brought food."

Piper started out of the closet. Great. Food. Too bad that wasn't what she was starved for.

8

---

*R*aider kept his eyes closed as he relaxed on the couch. Denlo paced in and out of the room constantly checking on them. While his downtime wasn't sleep, it was a rest of sorts. Raider was bone tired, and it had nothing to do with his current lack of sleep from the time spent helping with the evacuation of unfortunate citizens. This exhaustion was a direct result of Piper's ability to tie him up in knots. Even after the half decade since their split, he still wanted her. Wanted *them*.

He'd thought he'd finally gotten over her but now he knew he'd only been hiding from the truth. Judging by the speed of his reaction to her in the closet, Piper still owed his heart and the rest of him. The instant she'd kissed him, the sweet familiar taste of her had driven from his mind everything except his need to have her. Fuck, he couldn't allow that to happen again. This was his heart he needed to protect.

Denlo came into the room again, grunted at them, and then turned to leave. He'd done it so many times, Raider recognized the sound of his walk as well as the fact that his agitation was growing worse as time went by. Denlo stressed out wasn't something he wanted to witness. Especially since he had possession of the only gun in the house. Raider bit back a harsh chuckle as he considered the woefully insignificant knife still tucked into his boot. He muttered something about knives and gun fights under his breath as Denlo's steps rang on the marble floor.

There was more to this whole op than met the eye. He wanted immediate answers but forced himself to be content to let things play out a little while longer.

Reality was, Denlo was the least of his worries. The guy's lack of professional training could be used against him. The dummy didn't really know what the hell he was doing. Yes, he had a gun, but that was the only one he'd seen, and Raider didn't foresee that taking it from Denlo would be much of a problem. There was an element of risk involved, but after years of being a SEAL, Raider figured he had the jump on the guy in a situation involving hand-to-hand combat.

Instinctively, Raider kept his body as relaxed as possible. He needed Denlo to believe that he was sleeping and presented no threat. No need to have Denlo anymore on edge. The smell of toast reached him. The couch he'd claimed for his little nap that wasn't a nap was in the great room just around the corner from the kitchen. Denlo must be making himself a snack. Raider had noticed he hadn't eaten when the rest of them had, and he'd wondered. Now toast. Maybe he had a food issue? A nervous stomach that meant he couldn't eat anything but the stuff on the BRAT diet? Bananas, rice, applesauce, and toast. Imagine choosing against having a greasy fast food burger and fries, like the rest of them had. Pretty fucking boring, but whatever.

Wells and Baker were down the hallway in different rooms and Piper was in the primary bedroom. Denlo told her she could stay there but if she tried to exit the house he'd know about it because the house had an alarm which made a chirping sound if any door or window was opened. Piper had shot Raider a look but said nothing. She wasn't stupid. Denlo was making shit up and not thinking it through. How clueless did he think they were? They'd all been there and walked right into the house. Not one single alarm had sounded when they'd broken in. Raider had decided Denlo was worried about losing control of the group so he was making shit up to keep them from making a break for it. In this kind of situation, the best thing to do was to remain as passive as possible, hence pretending to sleep on the couch.

The sound of a phone ringing harshed his mellow. The call was answered immediately.

"'Bout time," Denlo snarled. There was silence and then he said, "Are you sure about the bank layout? The blueprints are wrong. Are you sure the vault is in the back corner?" Another silence. "My guy says they're wrong. That he should be seeing stuff on the shared wall and it's not there." Denlo must be pacing because he heard his footsteps scuffle closer and then recede again and again.

"We have to blow the hole in some office. The explosives guy says we can't do it at the front because it will blow the windows." Denlo had stopped pacing. By the sound of things, he was facing away from Raider in the kitchen. It was harder to understand what he was saying.

"You said you had this all figured out. You said..." Denlo's voice faded out. Then it was back, "police would be busy. I'm risking my neck for..." Denlo's voice dropped again. "Fine," he said. "But I'm telling you right now that if this all goes south, I'm not going down alone. It had better be there. I'm not breaking into any more banks looking for it. This is the last one." Denlo must've hung up because the conversation was followed by a long silence.

Interesting. So Denlo had broken into more than just this bank and he hadn't found what he was after. That fact begged the question; what is he looking for? And why do they think it is at this bank? Raider stopped to consider. It made sense. They were hitting a small bank, so likely there wasn't a ton of cash on hand. Breaking in was really all risk with little reward. If there was something else that Denlo and others wanted, that created a much different picture. They'd broken into multiple banks for whatever they were after, so it had to be valuable. Lots of ideas came to mind, but none of them jumped to the front screaming 'pick me.' God, this sucked.

Another question occurred to him: if money wasn't the target did that mean the team was getting paid from another source or not paid at all? Raider's gut told him it was the second scenario. Denlo probably had instructions to kill them all after the job was done. Could be one of the reasons Denlo was getting so agitated. Killing someone wasn't easy. Killing four someones with no backup was damn hard.

"Get up," Denlo snarled from across the room.

Raider pretended he was asleep.

"Get up," Denlo said coming closer. He kicked the couch and Raider opened his eyes like he'd been sound asleep. "Time to go." Denlo turned on his heel and stalked out of the room, going to wake everyone else.

Raider sat up. He'd left his boots on so he didn't have to find another place for the cell. Standing, he went down the hallway to the bathroom and locked the door behind him. He turned on the water in the sink and threw some on his face and hair, then pulled out the cell. He shot off a text to Harlan checking in and then he thought for a second and hit the call button. "Kian, did you find the guy?"

"Yeah, we got him. Wasn't easy but me and Waylen pulled him out."

"He's alive?" Raider asked.

"Barely. Not sure he's gonna make it. Dude, I don't know what you're involved in, but it doesn't look good from here."

"It's not," Raider agreed. He flushed the toilet and kept his voice low. "I need you to talk to Vardis, that's his name, and get details of the job from him. I don't have time to explain it now."

A loud bang on the door made Raider grit his teeth.

"Get the fuck out here," Denlo demanded.

"I'm taking a shit. Gimme a minute," Raider shot back. He dropped his voice. "I gotta go. Get

Vardis to explain everything. I'll call if I need help." He clicked off the call and stashed the cell in his boot, then flushed the toilet. Opening the door, he then leaned over and turned off the water.

Denlo glared at him. "What the hell were you doing in there?"

Raider cocked an eyebrow. "If I gotta explain it to you, then I think you got a problem."

"Just go get in the fucking van."

Raider crawled into the van and had to sit with Wells and Baker on the floor in the back. The van was stuffed with equipment for the job. Most of it was covered by a tarp so he didn't have a visual on the explosives or any of the stuff he needed but there were some power tools and rope exposed.

Once again, the idiocy of this struck him. Piper should know better. He got that she felt responsible for Marta's death but risking her life, and now his, wasn't the answer. He shifted as they drove, trying to get comfortable. He was risking his freedom for this. Breaking into a bank was no small thing and with no support from the outside, no one from the ATF backing them up, it was a hell of a gamble. He glanced at Piper. What the hell was he thinking? He was risking his freedom and his life for a woman who'd kicked him out without a backward glance. And who had yet to explain why. He needed his head examined.

No…what he needed was to get out of this.

They were approaching the intersection across from the bank. Denlo snarled, "Fucking hell." From Raider's angle, he couldn't see anything. He was behind Denlo's seat, so his view was of Piper and Wells who was sitting across from him.

Baker mumbled a curse and his eyes widened. Raider nudged him and raised an eyebrow. Baker just glanced at Denlo and shook his head slightly.

"Park over there at the dentist's office," Denlo instructed.

Piper made a left and then another left and pulled into the lot across from the strip mall. Raider had no view, but since she kept driving so he assumed she'd gone to the other end of the parking lot before turning around and facing the strip mall.

"Fuck," Denlo snarled again. "Okay, all of you stay here." He turned and his head came between the two seats. "If any of you moves from this van, I will hunt you down and kill you." He then hopped out of the van and slammed the door.

Raider waited all of fifteen seconds before saying, "What's going on?"

Baker shifted closer to Wells. "See for yourself."

Raider leaned forward. The entire parking lot of the strip mall was filled with emergency vehicles with their lights flashing. Cops, fire trucks, ambulances. They were all parked at varying angles, from the entrance by the convenience store and all the way down to the bank. Denlo jogged across the street and approached the convenience store.

Raider didn't bother to hold in the laughter. "Like this job wasn't fucked up enough already." Jesus, what else could go wrong? "They're using the parking lot as a staging area," Raider said to Wells.

The other man's eyes widened. "Shit."

"Yeah," Baker agreed. "This isn't good."

"None of this is good," Wells blurted. "Man, I am getting real cold feet about this job. I think we should run."

Raider tossed a glance at Piper. She looked over her shoulder and bit her lip as she met his gaze.

Baker suddenly nodded. "I'm with him. This is bad. I think we get the hell out of here. With all the confusion from the eruption, it should be easy to just disappear."

Raider looked out through the windshield. Denlo was talking to the same clerk who'd been behind the cash register the other night. Various cops and firemen milled about in the convenience store. One of them moved over to stand next to Denlo and started talking to him.

"If we're going, now's the moment." Raider looked at Piper.

She glanced back at him and then Baker. Then she gave a slight nod. Raider felt his shoulders unknot just a fraction. Piper cranked the engine and started slowly forward, heading down the parking lot away from the store. She made it almost to the street when Denlo saw them through the glass. He raced out of the store to the parking lot with the cop not far behind. Piper hit the gas and turned onto the street. She zoomed through the intersection and took a right. They continued to drive in silence for about ten minutes before Piper finally said, "Make the call."

"What call?" Wells asked.

Raider pulled the cell out of his boot.

"You've got a cell?" Baker stared at him as he turned the cell on and hit re-dial.

"It's me."

"Me who?" the voice at the other end barked. "Wait, Raider is that you?"

"Yeah."

"Is Piper okay?"

"Yeah." Raider knew Chambers had always had a soft spot for Piper. He'd sensed it when he and Piper were still a couple. He didn't worry about it at the time because John Chambers was at least ten years older with a large belly and a lot of kids. But now, the concern in his voice made Raider wonder. Maybe he should've worried more about Chambers.

"Where are you?" Chambers demanded.

"We're headed out of Hilo. Where are you?"

"At a small office building about two miles down from your motel. What's going on?" he asked.

Raider glanced at Piper. "Just give me directions and we'll explain it all when we get there. There's four of us."

"You're bringing along the other two guys?"

"Not much choice," Raider confirmed. He listened to the directions and gave them to Piper then hung up.

"What's going on," Wells demanded. "Who are you two?"

Piper swung into the parking lot of an older office building and drove around back. She threw the van into park and got out. Raider reached up and opened the van door, to find three men standing there, guns out pointing in his direction. He slowly raised his hands and swung his legs out of the van. He stood. "Hey, John," he said to the older man standing behind the line of guys.

"Raider," Chambers replied then instructed the armed men, "Let him by." Then he tipped his chin toward the building.

Raider followed Piper and Chambers into the building to an office space where three other agents of varying ages and nationalities were hunched over computers. None of them spared much more than a cursory glance at him, but each had a smile for Piper.

Wells and Baker were brought and put in another office. One of the agents stayed with them and the other two returned to the main room.

Chambers stared at Piper with a look on his face that told Raider the older man wanted to rip her a new asshole. But he must have recognized that now wasn't the moment. Instead, he said, "Coffee?"

Raider nodded. Piper went over and poured them two cups from the makeshift setup in the corner of the office. She handed Raider his and then followed Chambers to a cubicle that was obviously his version of command and control. There was a laptop on the desk and papers everywhere. Although it looked chaotic, Raider could tell there was a method to the madness.

Chambers sat. "We're trying to figure out how much money is in the bank and why these guys would target it."

"It's not about the money," Raider supplied.

Piper turned and stared at him.

"I overheard Denlo on the phone earlier.

They've broken into a couple other banks looking for something. Whoever he's working with thinks whatever it is, it's in this bank. Denlo's starting to lose it. The stress is getting to him. He was threatening whoever was on the other end of the phone. He said this is his last job so what they were after had better be here."

"Well shit," Chambers said. "That puts a new spin on things. Collins," Chambers bellowed. A young guy hurried around the corner. He was wearing a button-down with a pair of jeans and he looked to be in his mid-twenties. Raider stared. When had everyone gotten so damn young? The kid had been one of the agents on the computer when they'd come in, probably the computer geek of the lot. Had to be young to keep up these days. He had no idea how Waylen did it.

Chambers pointed at him. "I need a list of bank robberies here and in the whole US in the last six months. See if you can find any pattern or if anything weird sticks out."

"On it," the kid said and disappeared around the upholstered wall that created Chambers' cubicle.

"What else can you tell me," Chambers demanded.

"Not much," Piper said. "All I know is we were supposed to rob a bank."

"So why are you here?" Chambers asked.

She shrugged. "Denlo was starting to unravel. The whole job feels...off."

"It's too fast," Raider supplied. "From what I can gather, they changed the timeline. I think they were planning on it doing a couple of weeks down the road." He looked to Piper who nodded her agreement. "But when the volcano blew, they decided to move up the op. It's pretty smart. All the first responders would be busy elsewhere and honestly if the bank alarm went off, it would be a second priority to getting people out of harm's way."

Chambers leaned back in the chair. "So why are you here?"

Piper sighed. "Because Denlo seemed to be losing it and none of us thought the job was going to work and the whole thing gave us a bad feeling."

Chambers looked back and forth between Piper and Raider. "So what? You thought pulling the plug was a good idea? Goddammit, Piper, you jumped on a plane with no backup, got involved in this mess without approval, and now you want to just let it go? I've gone to the mat for you on this. You can't just pull the plug now."

Raider had the urge to punch Chambers. "What the hell was she supposed to do? Wasn't like you had everything under control on your end. She's out there on her own. It's dangerous."

"I thought you were there to help her," Chambers shot back.

Raider leaned forward in his chair. "She jumped on a plane and you left her hanging out there. She had no idea what level of readiness you're at and Denlo is starting to fall apart. The situation is volatile and, like the fucking volcano, this can blow up at any minute. She came in because she was in danger. This thing looked like it was turning south."

Chambers' face was a dull red. "I did the best I could within the time frame I was given. Piper never should've gotten on the plane, but she did, and now we're here. She needs to go through with this so we can nail this guy and find out what the hell is really going on. This could be our only line to Marta's killer."

Raider couldn't believe his ears. What a line of bullshit. He knew Chambers had put his ass on the line for Piper but telling her to go back in was just batshit crazy. He leaned forward to tell Chambers just what he thought when there was a commotion behind him. He turned to see a man in a suit arrive along with two other suited agents.

"Who the hell is that?" Raider asked.

"Tom Fielding," Chambers grumbled as he stood and then walked out of the cubicle.

Piper watched Chambers meet and shake hands with Fielding. She met Raider's gaze. "He's the Assistant head of the field operations group. So Chambers' boss's boss's boss."

"What the hell is he doing here?"

Piper shrugged "No idea, but whatever's up won't be good."

Raider's stomach rolled. He'd thought he'd gotten Piper out of harm's way and that now she'd be safe, except his gut told him, she was still in trouble. The way things were going, he might not be able to save her this time.

9

*P*iper didn't know which was worse. Raider who so obviously wanted to flatten John, or John who was completely oblivious and kept not so subtly threatening her. She sighed and stood. She had no interest in talking to Fielding. By all accounts, he was a flipping blowhard who was great at the political stuff but not so good at doing the actual work.

"Piper," John called and waved her over. She stood and moved around Raider to go stand with John and Fielding.

"Agent Holloway. Nice to meet you." Fielding cast a disdainful eye over her ratty blond hair and her dirty clothes.

Yeah, she wasn't looking her best but that's what undercover was like. Of course, his look made her want a shower even more. "Assistant

Director Fielding," she greeted him with a nod. She might look like hell, but she wasn't going to let him run over her. *Keep it professional, Piper.*

He glanced around the room. "Is there somewhere we can talk, John?"

Chambers nodded and led the way out of the main room. Fielding followed him, walking like an overrated jock on the football field. Piper trailed behind and wondered what Raider thought of the man. He'd always had good instincts. Chambers proceeded down a hallway to a small office. Fielding entered, ushered Piper in like he owned the damn place, and then closed the door. He sat behind the desk. John ushered Piper to the guest chair by the wall and he sat down beside her. She had the instant impression that she had been cornered.

Whatever was coming wasn't going to be good.

"So, John was telling me how you got here and I have to say it was a pretty ballsy move getting on that flight. Some might call it insubordinate." He let his gaze rest on her face.

She fought the urge to justify her actions. Instead, she just said, "Yes, sir." He wasn't here to yell at her, at least not yet. He didn't fly out here in his pristine white shirt and light gray business suit with a white pinstripe to tell her she'd screwed up. He was here for something else. If she kept quiet, eventually he'd get around to telling her what that something was.

"John assures me you are one of his best agents." He looked skeptical of John's opinion of her. "I understand you lost your partner in the warehouse debacle. I am truly sorry. We're still working on finding out how that guy got inside without us knowing."

She merely nodded. His statement didn't require a response.

"So, you came in without bringing in the leader, this guy named Denlo. Why is that?" Fielding narrowed his pale blue eyes at her. His dark blond hair was neat, and his skin looked sun-kissed. The perfect picture of an understanding, experienced ATF agent. He was just there to hear what she said, nothing more. That's what the look said…but that's not what he really meant. He wanted to know how she could've pulled the plug on the op at this stage.

"Sir, Denlo was starting to fall apart. He was getting more and more agitated. It was only a matter of time before he killed someone." And she sure as hell hadn't wanted to be the person on the receiving end of all his crazy. Her or Raider.

"I see," Fielding said. But clearly, by the look of his pursed lips, he didn't. "You felt you were in danger."

"Yes." And she had. Moreover, and more

importantly, she thought Raider might be in danger because if anyone was going to challenge Denlo it would be her ex-husband and the idea that he might get hurt on her watch was just untenable. She wouldn't survive it. She owed Marta but she wouldn't sacrifice Raider for her deceased colleague.

Fielding spared a glance at her boss and then redirected his focus to her. He leaned back in the chair and said, "What if I were to tell you that we know that Denlo is actually pretty low on the totem pole? That he's merely answering to someone else...the man who killed your partner probably, but even that guy answers to someone else. That this whole op is much bigger than you thought?"

She blinked. Snake wasn't the top guy? That was an interesting thought. "How much bigger?"

Fielding's lips curved up at the corners. "A lot. We think you and Agent Grant stumbled onto the tip of the iceberg. A group has been shipping guns in and out of the US for some time now. Fueling an assortment of terrorist groups with weapons from our own military." He sneered in disgust. "We have a gang problem in the military and they're stealing equipment and selling it to our enemies. What you and Agent Grant came across was the tip of that. We've been working it from another angle for months now. Our other operation has ferreted out that there's a small group at the top running the whole show and that your op is just one arm of it." He paused to let that sink in.

Piper cocked her head. What he was saying made sense. They'd suspected there was something bigger going on because the size of the deals made by the criminals they were following were way too big for what they should be. Snake being part of a much larger operation made sense.

"So do you know who the top people are?"

"Not yet. But we do know that the reason Denlo wants you to break into the bank isn't about money. Apparently, someone kept a record of all the deals. The person in question is dead but the record is still out there in the form of a USB drive. Rumor has it that the drive is at the bank that Denlo wants you to break into. That's why he's desperate. If anyone but the inside people find that information, the whole operation comes crashing down."

A cautionary shiver crept along Piper's nerves. The info was all too vague. "And how do you know all this if you don't know who's at the top of the food chain? Do you know who created the list?"

"We have our sources." Piper must have had a misbelieving look on her face because Fielding relented. "We have a man on the inside. We do know the identity of who kept track and created the list. But that lead turned into a dead end when his body washed up in San Diego a couple of months ago. The thing is, he'd just finished traveling to all kinds of places when he popped up and there's been a mad search ever since to locate the thumb drive. We now believe that that documentation is inside that bank. Or at least that's what Denlo and whoever his immediate boss believes. We also have reason to believe the drive contains a list of names. A holy grail of who is breaking the law by allowing these gangs to sell American technology and weaponry. Our understanding is that we will find some high-ranking officials on the list as well as law enforcement and politicians."

Piper's stomach rolled. A list like that would be a gold mine for the ATF, but the number of people that would want it buried would be huge as well. Anyone who'd actually seen the list was in a very dangerous position.

Including her now. He'd all but just hung a target on her back. "Why are you telling me all this," she asked, doing a piss-poor job of keeping dread from her voice.

"Because"—he nodded at John—"we want you to go back in. We need you to break into the bank like Denlo wants. We need that thumb drive and you're going to get it for us."

Piper's heart stopped, then thumped harshly to restart. They wanted her to go back. They were willing to risk her life to get this thumb drive. She'd gotten out because she'd felt the situation had been unsafe, and now they wanted her embedded with a crazy man again. Not a care in the world for her safety, or Raider's. Fielding had all but said this thumb drive was more important than her life. *Shit.*

"I'm not sure how I can make that work," she said finally. Even though she accepted that she had no real options, here, she tried to buy time to decide how much of a death wish she really had.

"You and the others would have to go back," Fielding said. He implied that it would be easy but what in the hell could they tell Denlo, and how would she convince the others to join the party?

"You make it sound easy, but I don't think it's that simple. Why would he trust any of us now?"

Fielding nodded. "I know it might seem daunting, but I think we've devised a plan that might work. You're going to tell Denlo you got spooked but now you're good and you just want to get the job done."

She snorted. It was an asinine plan that didn't have a hope in hell of working. They'd need a better story than that. She glanced at John expecting him to share his thought process but his face was impassive and…what the hell?…he was nodding slightly. Was he for real? No way would that stupid ass plan work. Plus, she'd need the whole team.

"How are we going to get Wells and Baker to do what they're told?" It seemed an obvious issue, but she thought she'd better bring it up since they seemed to have very limited understanding of how this would work in the real world.

John cleared his throat. "Our guys are telling them if they don't cooperate then they'll spend the rest of their lives at a black site and talking to no one but the CIA."

She frowned. "What? Why would they believe that?"

Fielding leaned forward. "Because we can tie the guns to terrorism, and they are being told that the money in the bank is proceeds from the sale of said guns and they are now an accessory after the fact."

"But that's all bullshit," Piper exploded.

John shrugged. "Yes, but they don't know that. They'll believe whatever we tell them. Honestly, I don't think they care," he added. "They don't want to go to jail. We tell them if they help us then we'll take prison off the table. And would you look at that... they'll be on board.

That whole scenario made the hair on Piper's arms stand up. Didn't sit right at all. There was so much that could go south here. Wells and Baker, although would-be bank robbers, weren't really bad guys. They kept to themselves and just wanted to make money. Stringing them along with the idea that they'd be dropped into a black site seemed underhanded.

"Let me get this straight… You want to send me in with two guys who could blow my cover at any moment," she stated baldly. She wanted it on the record that her boss was overriding her worries. Of course it wasn't really on the record. John and Fielding were acting more like Pete and Re-Pete on this one. Just two peas in the damn pod.

John shook his head. "I think we were clear, Piper. These guys don't want to go to jail so they won't say anything. Honestly, I think it's a bit of a relief for them. Denlo is scary to them and now they know the ATF is backing them up, so there's less chance of them getting hurt."

Piper shook her head. "What if I don't want to go back in?" she asked, testing the waters.

John glanced at Fielding, who said, "I guess if you really feel that you can't do it, then we'll have to live with your decision. But declining this opportunity means you'll never get justice for Marta. You'll be walking away from the one chance we have to get these bastards. I, for one, would hate to miss this opportunity. Our fallen colleagues deserve justice." He looked at her like she was worse than pond scum for even thinking about walking away. Heaving an exaggerated sigh, he frowned. "There's also the question of your insubordination. I'm sure you'll have to answer for that at some point but it would go much better if you helped bring down this criminal enterprise."

Bile filled Piper's mouth. There it was. The cold unvarnished truth. Do this or you're going to be drummed out of the ATF. Maybe even face jail time herself, likely in the same prison she'd sent many, many villains to. A blue streak of curses was on repeat in her head.

It was her own fault though. Why the hell had she gotten on that airplane?

"Of course, Raider will have to go with you. Denlo needs an explosives expert, and we can't just pop a new one in, it would be way too suspicious," John added.

So not only was she supposed to risk her own life, she would risk Raider's too. Wells and Baker could open their mouths and Denlo would kill them all. Her heart pounded in her ears as adrenaline hit her veins. What she had here was a really bad hand. And she'd dealt it to herself. Now she was going to have to go back in there and deal it to Raider.

She stood. "It's not just my decision. I have to talk to Raider and Wells and Baker. I'll not put Raider in harm's way if I don't think Wells and

Baker will keep their mouths shut. Raider is a civilian."

"Hardly a civilian," John said. "He's a Navy SEAL. He's got more experience at this type of thing than most of the guys in that office combined."

"But he's not ATF." Piper pointed out. "And this is an ATF operation."

John opened his mouth but Fielding waved him off. "Fine, go talk to him. See what he says. But the clock is ticking. We can't leave Denlo hanging out there. The longer you're gone, the harder it will be to get him to believe you when you return."

Piper glared at John until he moved out of the way and then she left the office. This was bullshit, all of it. Her gut told her something else was going on, but it didn't matter. She no longer had a choice and now she had to tell Raider he didn't have one either. This wasn't going to go well.

She found him sitting where she'd left him. She asked one of the guys to bring them coffee and once they had their cups, she took him outside to the back parking lot and sat down on the bumper of the van.

"They want you to go back in," Raider said before she'd even had a chance to open her mouth.

She nodded. "They say that this is the tip of a

very large weapons dealing ring involving terrorist organizations and our military. Fielding says that the ATF has a man on the inside in a secondary op. The thing Denlo and Snake are after is a thumb drive with a list of the sales, buyers, and sellers, as well as a list of government officials involved."

Raider whistled. "So a who's who of corruption and arms deals. Excellent."

"Yeah." She took a sip of coffee to stall. "They say this is the only chance they have to get this list."

Raider stared at her. "You're going to do it? You're going to go back in? But Wells and Baker have to go, too."

"According to John and Fielding, the two are so scared of going to jail that they've agreed to keep their mouth shut."

Raider snorted. "I don't believe that for a second."

"Apparently, they've been told that this involves terrorist organizations and if they don't cooperate, they'll be dropped in a CIA black site."

"For shit's sake, what kind of idiot would believe that?" Raider demanded.

Piper glanced up at her ex. "Those two strike you as smart?"

Raider stared at her and then sighed. "I guess not." He shook his head. "What's the plan?"

She frowned. "You don't have to do this. I called you because I was desperate, and I needed help but now John is here and Fielding. We can find another explosives guy."

"This only works if we all go back. Denlo won't buy it any other way." Raider stared into his coffee. "Why don't they just round Denlo up and then go into the bank and look for themselves?"

Piper laughed. "Spoken like a SEAL. There are search and seizure laws we have to abide by. We need probable cause for a warrant. We can't just go in and search the bank. Plus, we don't know anything about the thumb drive and from what I've gathered, no one has seen it, so we're not even positive it exists. No way can we just stroll in there and search the entire bank for something we don't know who owns and we can't even say for sure exists." She grinned. "Must be nice being a SEAL and waltzing in anywhere you want."

"Except for the whole I was behind enemy lines worried about getting my ass shot off thing, so yeah, not worrying about a warrant was great fun."

The sarcasm hit her hard and she immediately felt like shit. "I'm sorry. That was a stupid thing to say." Her breath rushed out. "Wait, you said was."

"What?" Raider asked.

"You said 'I *was* behind enemy lines'." She stared up at him.

Raider grimaced. "I retired about six months ago."

"Holy shit. Seriously?" Piper had a hard time comprehending what Raider was telling her. "You retired?"

"Yeah, and I've got to say so far retired life isn't living up to the hype. Too boring."

Piper burst out laughing. Of all the things she thought would happen, Raider retiring wasn't one of them. He just couldn't stand not doing something. He needed to be moving constantly.

"Probably would be a lot less bored if we'd stayed married and had a couple kids by now." Raider studied his boots.

Guilt rose like a ready-to-strike cobra. The pain in her chest made her feel like it had already sunk its fangs into her. She'd always figured when he got out, he'd go into something else right away. Any law enforcement agency would kill to have a guy with his kind of experience.

She forced a laugh. "I don't know, I can't imagine changing diapers would be your cup of tea."

He looked up sharply and scowled. "I'm glad you think it's funny. You know how much I wanted that life," he said, his voice cold.

She stood up and touched his arm, looking for

a graceful way out of this conversation. "I'm sorry, Raider. I just never pictured you retired. You hate doing nothing. Wait, no! Tell me you didn't take up golf?"

He shrugged. "I've played a few rounds. Damn boring if you ask me but the guys seem to like it."

"All the guys retired too?"

He nodded. "We all requested permission to go ashore at the same time. It's what's been keeping me sane. Hanging with them and traveling around the world."

Piper sobered up. She'd put this man through hell and he was still standing there ready to help her. She didn't deserve that kind of loyalty and support. "Thank you," she said in a quiet voice. "You came when I needed you. I owe you."

He grabbed her chin. "I'll do this on one condition. When this is over, you're going to tell me the real reason you kicked me to the curb. The whole truth."

She held his gaze and bit her lip. That was the last thing she wanted to do. He'd hate her probably more than he already did, but he was right. She owed him the explanation. "Fine," she breathed, grateful for his help, and the short respite she'd have before having to unbury her secret. She swallowed hard to keep from tearing up. "Deal."

"Now we need to go in and get Wells and Baker on board. Then we need to get back to Denlo and somehow convince him that we didn't run out on him." Raider dropped his hand from her chin, and she shivered with the loss. He squared his shoulders. "I've got some ideas about that." With that, he turned and headed for the door.

Piper watched him go. This whole thing was a clusterfuck of her own making. All of it. What had happened, and then the divorce, getting Marta killed... All of it was on her. And now the chickens were coming home to roost. Karma was a bitch that was coming for her like a freight train.

10

*R*aider hurried down the hallway until he found an empty office. He went in, closed the door, and pulled the burner cell phone from his boot. He dialed a number and waited.

"Yo," the voice came down the line.

"Lane, it's Raider."

"Raider, I don't have a lot of time, what's up?"

"I'll be quick. Piper is doing an undercover thing and I got dragged into it—"

"Aw hell, you okay?"

The urge to say hell no welled up in him. He wasn't okay but now wasn't the time to get into all the touchy-feely shit romping through him. "It's fine. Listen, there's a group of weapons dealers operating in the US. Apparently, they're huge and moving some serious equipment. Including stolen military stuff. You hear anything about this? Have any ideas about it?"

Lane whistled. "I've heard rumors. No one says too much, and when they crack open their yaps about it, they only whisper it when no one is around. Whoever is behind it has serious high up government pull. Think top-level decision-makers. This is not the stuff you want to get involved in. Retired means not getting involved."

Raider grinned. "And what are you doin' right now? I saw how you shot out of the room when that woman was on the screen. You lit up like a Christmas tree. Dude, retired means choosing *when* to get involved."

"Christmas tree?" Lane snorted. "Asshole."

Raider's grin broadened. "So, do you know anything helpful?"

"Yeah, stay out of the way and don't get shot."

"Right. I hadn't thought of that. Thanks." Raider chuckled. "Seriously though, you know anything?"

"Nothing concrete other than their complete lack of fear or hesitation over taking out anyone who creates problems for them. Just be careful. It's a big network. My best advice; trust no one"

"Thanks, Lane. I hope Christmas comes early for you." Lane hung up swearing.

Raider smiled. Calling the guys always helped him. Even if they had no new information, just touching base made him feel like he was in control, whether that was the truth or not.

He looked around the sparsely furnished office. There was nothing in it. Just an old desk and a chair. He sat and took stock of his attitude. He was a mess, no question. Seeing Piper had thrust him back a few steps, but holding her and kissing her had rocked his world. The path ahead would be long and dark if he let himself go down that particular rabbit hole again. He'd be better served to cut off one of his own limbs than to try to chase that dream again. God knew he'd tried to move on. There'd been other women. But none had measured up to Piper. He'd never seen a future with anyone else. Only Piper. And look where that landed him: right in the middle of a goddamn shit show.

Swearing, he leaped up from the desk. Focus on getting the job done and then getting the hell away from Piper was the name of the game. He wouldn't let her go in alone because chances were excellent that Denlo would kill her but the second this was over, he would get his answer and then he'd get as far from Piper as he could. Answers would give him closure, and the ability to get on with his life.

Twenty minutes later he joined Piper, Wells, and Baker in the van. Piper was driving with Raider in the passenger seat. He looked at his watch. Two a.m. The job wouldn't happen tonight which was a good thing because the delay gave Chambers a chance to properly set up for the coming op. He seemed to have no issue with resources now that Fielding was on site.

"So, are you two okay with everything?" Piper asked.

"Okay?" Baker asked. "No, not even close but what choice do we have?"

Raider grimaced. This was less than ideal circumstances, to say the least. "Look at it this way, you weren't comfortable with the job in the first place. Now you have the support and protection of the ATF. Denlo isn't going to be able to kill you. You just have to go through the motions on this job and then you'll be good to go."

Wells grunted. "Good to go until the ATF shows up and arrests us out of the blue. I don't trust you guys. You'll screw us eventually."

Piper glanced in the rearview mirror. "I won't let that happen. I promise I'll do my best to protect you and get you out once this is over."

God, he wished she'd stop over-promising. At delivery time, it could get hairy.

She continued, "Then my best advice is run far and run fast. The ATF won't bother to follow you right off. You can get away and just disappear."

Raider glanced over his shoulder at Baker and

Wells who were exchanging looks. "She's telling you the truth. Denlo was always going to kill us once the job was done. He doesn't have a choice. We can all identify him and this job isn't what he's saying it is, so we're loose ends. The people in charge aren't going to want us around." Raider wondered if whoever was in charge would want Denlo around. Would be easy to kill him too. Then the trail stops cold if anyone looked into the bank robbery.

"So, what's the plan?" Baker asked, sounding resigned.

Raider shrugged. "We're gonna go back to the house we broke into. It's been a few hours since we left Denlo. I'm guessing we should make it back there before him but not by much."

Wells huffed, "Why would he go back there?"

"Because it's the last place we were all together and his ass is on the line. Remember that he has to go through with this job. He needs to know if we really all ran off or did something else happened. Chances are good he will be totally freaking out by the time we meet up. He needs us way more than we need him, but he doesn't want us to realize that."

The smell of the burgers they'd stopped to pick up at the all-night drive-through had Raider's stomach growling. They'd bought one for Denlo not that anyone had seen him eat anything, but they thought it would help sell their story. Piper turned onto the street they'd been on earlier but no sign of Denlo. He was probably working his way through the woods. Piper turned up the drive and came to a stop outside the front door. The guys all got out and she lined the van up with the garage door. Raider sent Wells around to open it for her, while he and Baker set up the food on the dining room table.

Raider was jonesing to search the house, but there was a niggling worry that if he looked too professional Denlo would get suspicious. Instead, he got the food sorted and they all started eating.

Maybe twenty minutes into their mostly silent meal, a sharp knock sounded on the sliding glass doors to the backyard. Startled, Wells swore and then blanched.

Denlo was on the patio, gun drawn and looking wild as he shifted from one foot to the other like he needed to piss like a racehorse.

Raider felt rather than saw that Baker and Wells had tensed up.

"Okay," he said in a quiet voice. "You can do this. Our lives depend on it." He sauntered over and slid the door open. Denlo came flying into the room.

"What the fuck did you think you were doing?" he bellowed, waving the gun at Piper. "You bitch! You left me there!"

Raider had gone back over to the kitchen and now stood behind the counter next to Piper. "Calm the fuck down," he ordered. "Yelling will attract attention. We don't want that."

Denlo swung the nine-millimeter in his direction. "Shut up, asshole! No one is talking to you." He swung the barrel back toward Piper. "What the fuck?" Denlo demanded.

She frowned. "We saw you."

"You saw me? What the fuck does that mean? You saw me?" Denlo was waving the gun all around. Spittle collected in the corners of his mouth. His eyes were darting all around, lighting on nothing in particular.

Piper kept her voice calm and even. "In the convenience store. We saw you talking to the cashier guy and then the cop came up to you. We all thought you were getting busted. I mean it was crazy as hell to go in there with all those cops around. Then when we started to roll and you came outside, the cop came out with you. We figured we were all dead in the water then. If he got all of us, then the job was not gonna happen. It seemed like taking off was the smartest course of action."

Denlo came across the room and put the gun up to Piper's temple. "I want the truth, bitch or I put a bullet in your brain."

Raider wanted to knock the gun from Denlo's

hand and throttle the man, but he'd always trusted Piper's instincts and when she flashed out her hand on the counter, he took it as a sign that she had this. He adjusted his position next to her, to where he'd have a good angle at striking the man's temple to knock him off balance. He'd give her the space she needed but would stand ready, just in case.

Piper's throat worked, like she was swallowing hard, but she managed to keep her voice neutral. "I am telling you, we thought you were getting busted. All of us getting busted wouldn't have helped our cause."

"I don't believe you," Denlo snarled.

"It's— It's the truth," Baker said with a slight tremor in his voice. "We—we could see through the window into the convenience store and those cops were all over you. We thought for sure you were getting busted. We figured we would come back here and wait for you. If you didn't show, then we'd all go our separate ways."

Piper's hand shook slightly but she kept her voice sounding smooth, even a little bored. "We did think—"

Denlo took a step back and waved the gun at the whole group. "You fuckers. If I find out you're lying to me, I'll kill every one of you. And it won't be quick or painless."

Piper nodded. She glanced at Wells and Baker. They nodded too.

"We're telling the truth," Wells said as he ran a hand over his head. "Honest to God, it looked like you were getting busted. We have a van full of equipment to rob something big, including explosives. We did not want to get caught with that kind of contraband, but we came back to meet you. We're still up for the job."

Denlo's narrowed his eyes, the squint making him look deadly. "From now on, you all are going to do every fucking thing I say when I say it, understand?" He pointed the gun at Piper. "You understand," he said to her and then turned to Raider. "Do you understand? Because if any one of you screws up in any way, she dies. Are we clear?"

Although his stomach was pitching toward his boots, Raider nodded. Only years of training for these kinds of lethal scenarios kept him from reaching across the counter and snapping the asshole's neck. He'd play along. *For now.* There might come a point where playing along wasn't going to work any longer. The ATF would just have to live with those consequences because if this guy kept threatening Piper this way, Raider wasn't sure he could contain himself.

Denlo gave one final glare to the entire group and then grabbed the bag of food off the counter. Glancing inside he swore. "Go get some sleep. We can't do the job tonight. Don't even think about going anywhere." He put the food bag back on the counter. "Give me the van keys."

Piper handed over the van keys. Raider wasn't pleased but he wasn't as bothered since the ATF now knew where they were and if they needed help they should be able to get it. Plus there was always his burner cell phone. He'd tucked it back in his boot and breathed a bit easier knowing they had that out.

Still, being trapped here wasn't ideal.

"Now, get some sleep. We're doing this tomorrow night no matter what." Denlo put the gun in his waistband, grabbed the bag again, and stalked out of the room.

Wells and Baker looked at Raider, who cocked his head toward the hall Denlo had just rushed down. "Do what the man says. Get some sleep. Tomorrow night will come quickly and we're all gonna need to be on our game."

Baker nodded. Wells just shook his head. The two disappeared down the hall.

Piper turned to him. "Where are you going to sleep?"

"With you." The words were out before he even thought about them, but he knew it was true. There was no way in hell he was leaving Piper alone with Denlo being so on edge. One wrong move and that asshole would go ballistic.

Piper stared at him for a beat but then nodded. She went across the room and down the hall as well. The primary bedroom she'd used before was already occupied. So were the other two rooms with double beds. He followed her into the last room with a set of bunk beds with Star Wars comforters.

Piper slipped into the bathroom and Raider waited by the bunks. He'd let her take the inside. Easier to protect that way. He needed to be able to get up in a hell of a hurry and just the idea of being trapped on the inside gave him hives.

This whole situation had him on high alert. He hated not knowing what the hell was going on. Every instinct he possessed told him Fielding wasn't telling the whole truth. Chambers was just sucking up, as near as Raider could figure it. He overheard one of the young guys on the ATF team say that lately, Chambers was a real bear. Ever since his divorce was finalized. Maybe the guy was bucking for a promotion to help pay alimony? Would make sense. He shouldn't complain too much. Chambers had come through in the end and gotten people mobilized here on the Big Island. He owed the guy for that, and he'd obviously kept a close eye on Piper which was good. Since she didn't have Raider to do it, someone needed to.

Piper emerged from the bathroom and crossed the hall to the room, coming to a stop in the middle of the room. "So I guess we're sharing. Do you want top or bottom?"

So many things flooded his mind. All kinds of memories of various positions they'd tried. It damn near killed him not to grab her and kiss the daylights out of her. Instead, he cocked an eyebrow and said, "I seem to remember you like it on top."

Piper's cheeks flushed pink and she shook her head. "Seriously, Raider?"

He shot her a grin. "Doesn't matter what you like tonight. You're on the inside and I'll take the outside of the bottom bunk.

Piper put her hands on her hips. "Just wait a second. Are you telling me you think I can't take care of myself?"

"There is no way in hell you believe that I believe that." Raider advanced on her until he was close enough to catch a whiff of her scent. The citrusy floral combination that was distinctly hers. It had always played havoc with his senses and tonight was no exception. "I would never question your ability. But in this situation, we're better off… I'm telling you that I have your back.

There are too many uncontrollable variables here, and you need help."

She narrowed her eyes at him but took a step back. "Fine," she said and then turned and crawled onto the bunk. Raider waited until she was settled and threw the Star Wars comforter from the top bunk over her. Then, without removing his boots, he crawled in beside her. She was on her left side turned away from him. He'd sprawled out on his right side, so they were back to back. He'd feel a lot better if he had a gun but there was no way to risk it. If any situation arose, he'd just have to deal.

Having his back to Piper was the best option. If he turned and she curled up to him, he wasn't sure if he could stop himself from starting something. He was getting a hard-on as it was. He let out a sigh. It was going to be a long night.

11

Piper hoped the dream she was having never, ever ended. She was curled into Raider's arms and the sun was shining. Life was good and everything was right with the world. That's how she'd always felt when they'd been married. Right up to the day she sent him packing.

She drew in a deep breath. His scent surrounded her, so familiar and still capable of awakening every nerve ending in her body after all these years. She fought opening her eyes, because lifting her lids meant the world would intrude, and life would go on. Even as she squeezed them closed, she knew she had to face the facts. From some other corner of this house, she detected movement.

With a heavy sigh, she cracked one eye.

Raider was on his back and she was laying on the pillow next to him with her arm and leg over his hard body. Retirement hadn't softened his muscles in the least. His face looked relaxed and there was a hint of a smile on his lips. He must be dreaming of something good.

Maybe it was about her.

Probably not.

Not after what she'd done.

Five more minutes, she decided. Five more minutes of pretending and bliss until she let reality crash in. She'd allow herself that.

"Penny for 'em." Raider's voice rumbled his chest under her fingertips.

Damn him. He had always been able to fool her into thinking he was sleeping. "Just thinking about tonight." *Liar. Liar. Pants on fire.* "We should get up and see what's going on with the volcano."

"That's not what you were thinking about," Raider growled. "You were thinking about me."

His long, dark eyelashes remained on his cheek, his eyes closed but she frowned at him anyway.

"Don't bother to deny it and don't frown. It will give you wrinkles."

Now she really wanted to kill him. How had he known that without even opening his eyes?

Raider smiled. "You think loudly, and you've

been stroking my chest for the last twenty minutes."

"Shit," she muttered as she snatched her hand away.

He chuckled. "You miss me."

Her breath caught. He had no idea just how much. Five long years and her heart still hadn't recovered. This man had been, dammit, still was, her world. Raider remained the only man she'd ever wanted in *that* way. But he'd hate her the instant she revealed the reason behind her leaving. She couldn't be sure if the stab of grief in her chest was for what could have been, or what would be once he found out the truth. She cleared her throat. "You always did have an inflated sense of yourself."

He grinned. "It's only inflated if it's not true."

She smacked him on the shoulder and struggled to sit up. "Come on, we should get up and get moving."

Raider opened his eyes, grumbled that he was already *up* and quickly sat upright and planted a quick kiss on her lips. Then he tossed his feet over the side of the bed and trundled off to the bathroom.

And yeah, he was already up. Even from the side view, she knew his physical reaction was because of her, not something merely biological.

Piper stared at the closed door between them.

This op couldn't end fast enough. As much as she wanted to stay with the man, her sense of self-preservation demanded she get far away from Raider. Drawing breath around him was difficult. Being this close to him, in a bed, made her heart hurt too damn much.

Once this was over, she'd go back to her life and he'd go back to his. Retirement suited him. He would hang with the guys and make a new life for himself. A life that hadn't included her for five years. More, if she thought about their various missions and workloads.

She cocked her head and thought about what her retirement could look like. Maybe she could create a brand new life for herself. Leave San Diego. Maybe even leave the ATF. Fielding would love it is she handed in her resignation. That would allow them to sweep the insubordination thing under the rug and keep intact the ATF's sterling reputation. Never mind that John had been struggling to get resources before Fielding arrived. The more she thought about it, the more she was convinced that leaving the ATF was the right move. She could try for some other law enforcement agency. Most governmental agencies looked for investigative and field experience like hers. Maybe she'd move to Hawaii. It was beautiful here, well, minus the lava. She could certainly get used to it all.

An unsmiling Raider stepped out of the bath, and she rose. The two of them strolled out to the kitchen. Wells, Baker, and Denlo were watching TV in the great room. Raider poured them both coffee from the pot on the counter and they joined the rest of the group in front of the television, getting the latest update on the volcano.

"The lava flow is still strong. Looks like it might hit the highway sooner rather than later," Wells said catching them up.

Piper didn't look at Raider. Lava on the highway would make a fast retreat an impossibility. Not to mention that being cut off would make it harder to get help when and if they needed it. She hoped John would be on it.

Denlo shifted his weight in his chair and swore. He looked uncomfortable. "The cops and fire department have moved on. They aren't using the strip mall for staging anymore. We're going tonight. Be ready to leave here at ten." With that, he stood up and half walked, half staggered down the long hallway, slamming the door to the primary bedroom.

"What's up with him?" Piper asked.

Baker half-smiled. "The food didn't agree with him is all he said. I think he's not feeling great."

The rest of the day passed slowly. As the minutes trudged by, Piper found herself getting increasingly antsy. It was, in a way, torture to spend the day with Raider and not really be with him but she was determined to enjoy it. Once this was over, then she would never see him again. It was too painful. Too difficult. She would treat herself better and one of her gifts to herself was forgiveness. She would forgive herself but she knew he wouldn't ever forgive her so there was no point in ever seeing him again.

"Raider," she said as they sat in the bedroom, "I've got a bad feeling about this." And she did. Her stomach was doing flips. Her senses were jangling.

He studied her for a moment and then nodded. "My gut tells me something is going on that we don't know about. Some piece of the puzzle that we just aren't aware of. Does anything stand out to you?"

She shook her head. "I've been wracking my brain all day but I just can't put my finger on it. It's like it's on the edge of my consciousness but I just can't bring it in."

There was a loud bang on the door. "It's time," Denlo bellowed.

Raider was on his feet in an instant and pulled Piper off the bed. She started to move away but he held her tight and then bent down to whisper in her ear. "Piper, if things start to go south I need you to listen to me okay, and do exactly as I say." She opened her mouth to argue that she could take care of herself, but he waved her off. "This isn't about ego or our relationship. This is me, the Navy SEAL, telling you, the ATF agent, that if I tell you to do something just do it. I have more experience in volatile situations than you do."

She pulled back and looked up at her, searching his face. The truth of his words was written in his steely expression. He really was just watching out for her.

She gave a single nod because she was smart enough to know that if Raider told her to do something, his instructions were because he'd thought ten steps ahead and it was the right thing to do.

He held her gaze a second longer almost like he was going to say more but instead, he leaned in and lightly kissed her forehead. Then he let her go and went out the door. She followed slowly and met everyone in the kitchen.

Together, they climbed into the van, and twenty minutes later Piper parked behind the deserted strip mall.

Denlo turned to her. "You're coming in with us."

Piper froze. That hadn't been part of the original plan. "Er, but I thought I was supposed to be the lookout."

"We don't need a lookout," Denlo snapped. "This entire end of the island is empty. We're gonna need more hands on deck inside. You're coming."

She nodded but swore violently in her head. The point of this was for her to be on the outside. They were going to have agents in the van so when everyone came out and opened the door they'd be surrounded. She glanced at Raider. He gave a slight nod. Yeah, he knew this was bullshit and the change in plans was going to screw everything up, but they didn't have a choice. The tingling sensation on her back was closer to pins and needles as she climbed from behind the wheel. They'd been here not even five minutes and already things were falling apart.

This op was doomed. She was doomed. She felt it in her soul. Her only goal now was for her and Raider to make it out alive, but a sixth sense told her they were going to need a miracle.

12

---

*a*s Wells and Baker started hauling the equipment out of the van. Raider pitched in to carry some of the tools, specifically, anything to do with explosives he didn't let anyone else touch. It wasn't that the inert material could go boom with the slightest mishandling. His caution was in the interest of getting an exact inventory of what he had to work with. Within minutes, they'd hauled everything into the empty space next to the bank. Picking up a satchel of tools, Baker led the way down the stairs and into the storage area in the basement. Wells went next, followed by Raider and Piper. Denlo brought up the rear, grunting softly with each step down. The dude was in serious distress but fighting to mask the discomfort.

Raider was preoccupied with developing an

alternative exit strategy since the plan they'd made with Chambers was already off the table. The change in plans had left him and his ex-wife vulnerable.

With the original plan, it was hard for Denlo to start shooting. Piper would be outside and if he shot the guys inside then she'd take off or that's what they wanted him to think. With Piper inside with them, there was nothing to stop Denlo from shooting them as soon as he got what he came for.

Baker was preparing the extra lighting they'd need to see what they were doing. Wells was helping him. Raider climbed a ladder and studied the ceiling. He was surprised to find it was made with cement. If it was not reinforced concrete, as he'd been told, then it wasn't hard to blow it. He used the laser tape measure to mark his spots on the ceiling. He double-checked the blueprints for the office and then measured and remeasured. They only had one chance at this.

"Are you ready?" Denlo growled. He'd been standing in the corner watching all the activity. Piper was leaning on the wall of the staircase, ready to go in either direction.

Raider snorted. "You really don't want to rush me when we're dealing with explosives."

Denlo shot him a glare.

"I mean, I could hurry it up, but setting the charge one millimeter"—he pinched his thumb and forefinger together—"in the wrong direction could collapse the whole ceiling, burying us." Raider's measurement didn't need to be that precise, but he doubted Denlo knew that.

A concerned frown crossed Denlo's features and he backed deeper into the corner, casting anxious eyes to the ceiling. "Just—" he didn't finish the sentence as he waved his hand in the air.

Keeping his smile to himself, Raider took out the C4 and put it where he needed it to make the hole large enough for them all to get through. He attached the electrodes to the explosive and then spooled out the wire as he climbed down the ladder. He stood back and looked at his work. It was solid. It would work for sure. "Okay, I'm ready."

"Jesus, that took forever," Denlo crabbed.

As he dragged the ladder to the side, he directed the group, "Get in the stairwell." There was a lot of reinforced concrete implemented in stairwell design. This was the safest place for the whole group to shelter when the bomb detonated. Raider indulged in a quick fantasy about leaving Denlo under the explosives, but he squashed the desire and crossed the room to follow the rest of them up to the top of the stairwell.

"Everyone ready?" At their nods. He said, "Fire in the hole," and pressed the button on the detonator.

There was a soft concussive *whomp* chased by the crash of falling concrete and a cloud of dust swirled up the stairs. Denlo started coughing, his whole body shaking. He made them wait another minute or so and then started down the stairs. They entered the storage room. There was a pile of rubble on the floor and a neat roundish hole in the ceiling about three feet by three feet.

"Yes!" Denlo hissed.

Wells smiled and fist-bumped Baker.

"Get the ladder. We're good to go," Denlo directed.

"Careful where you step. The floor wasn't reinforced concrete, so there's no telling if it will hold after we blew a hole in it."

A couple minutes later, they'd assembled inside the bank. No alarms had gone off and it didn't appear like they'd disturbed anything. The office they'd come up in was small and they'd been damn lucky, Raider noted. Another few inches to the right and the desk would've fallen into the cellar, making it difficult to climb up into the bank. As it was, the sturdy metal desk had been shifted off kilter by the explosion. But the floor felt solid, so he had reason to hope it wouldn't cave under anyone's weight.

Raider left the office with the others and subtly nudged Piper to fall in behind him. Everyone fanned out, moving cautiously.

Wells headed toward the vault. "Well, shit on a shingle." He stood outside it and stared. "Hey, Denlo?" he said his voice cracking.

"What?" Denlo strode to his side.

Wells pointed. "This isn't the type of vault you said would be here."

Denlo frowned. "What?"

Turning to him with wide eyes and sweat beading on his forehead, Wells said, "This is the wrong vault. I can't crack this one."

Denlo stared at him. "What do you mean you can't crack it? I thought you were supposed to be some hotshot safe cracker. Just get it done."

Wells shook his head. "That's not how it works. This model is way beyond any of the tools I have here. I should've realized something was majorly wrong when Baker said the blueprints were off. This vault is smaller than the one on the blueprint and it's a lot more sophisticated."

Denlo staggered backward, eyes wide. "So just fucking get it open. We've got all night."

Wells shook his head again. "We could have a month of Sundays and I wouldn't have enough time. I need completely different tools and…" he stared at the round vault door, "and I don't know how to open this vault."

Denlo's face clouded over. He pulled the gun from his waistband. "You better fuckin' figure it out." He raised the gun and pointed it at Wells' forehead.

Wells put his hands up and shot a frightened glance at Raider and Piper.

Raider glanced around the bank. "Just wait a second, Denlo. If the vault is smaller than the plans, then let's go see what else is here. Maybe the safety deposit boxes aren't in the vault. Maybe we can get something from them. Just hang on and don't go off all half-cocked. Let's see what's here."

Denlo glared at him. Then he turned back to Wells. "You better hope he's right."

Raider started searching the offices. In the back corner across from the vault was another door. He tapped on it, please to find it was solid steel. This looked promising. He knew that Denlo wanted the safety deposit boxes but he couldn't let Denlo know he knew.

He called everyone over. "This is the safety deposit box room. Maybe there's jewelry and bonds and stuff in here. We could break into this and see."

Denlo ran a hand over the door and nodded. He turned to Wells. "Can you open this one?"

Wells glanced at Piper and then back at Denlo. He went up to the door. "I...I don't know what's in it."

"What do you mean?" Denlo demanded.

Wells shrugged. "I mean I have no idea if it's just a steel door with a bunch of locks or if there's iron bars inside that will drop into the floor if the door is tampered with."

Denlo went right up to Wells and pointed the gun an inch from his head. "You'd better get working then. We don't have all night. And if metal bars drop into the floor, I'm going to kill you." For emphasis, Denlo jammed the gun into Wells' temple.

Sweat dripped onto the barrel from Wells' face but he nodded. He pointed at some tools with a shaking hand and Baker handed them over.

Raider backed up and took Piper with him. Baker came back to stand next to them. They watched Wells for the next twenty minutes before Raider finally took pity on the guy. "Denlo, it might be easier for me to blow the door."

Denlo turned to him.

"This section of wall isn't load-bearing. I can blow an access hole here." He tapped the wall next to the steel door. "It will be a hell of a lot faster than this. The only issue is that some of the boxes inside might get damaged." It was a risk but Raider figured Wells was on borrowed time at this point. Denlo had been pacing back and forth with this gun down at his side and his finger on the trigger. Raider couldn't tell if the safety was on, but chances were good the man was just that negligent.

Baker cleared his throat. "That's a much better idea. I mean, then we get out of here much faster and we don't need to worry so much about being discovered." He licked his lips. "If we can't break into the vault then we should get what we can."

Denlo whirled around and stared at him.

Shit. Baker shouldn't have brought up the vault. The man knew it, too, because he started swallowing convulsively.

Raider opened his mouth to try and convince Denlo when Piper cut him off. "They're right. This whole job is a mess. The guy who's feeding you info has been wrong about everything. He sucks. He's the reason this isn't working. Might as well cut our losses and take what we can."

Denlo's gaze bounced from person to person, his mouth opening and closing like he was trying to make up his mind.

"At least we get something out of this if we blow the door," Raider commented. He didn't have a lot of C4 left but he could make it work. He had enough of everything else.

Finally, Denlo narrowed his eyes but nodded once. Raider landed on his feet when he dropped back into the basement and wasted no time collecting the explosives and the rest of the materials. Piper was waiting for him the in bank's office and took the equipment he handed her. Once he climbed to the top of the ladder and hoisted himself back into the bank, he hurried to the main lobby.

Five minutes later, the door was rigged.

"Move back into that corner," he suggested to Denlo, Wells, and Baker, waving to the safest spot in the open lobby. He kept Piper close to him under the pretense of needing her help to lay the wires. He guided her around the corner and into the office space.

He gave her a nod and called out, "Fire in the hole," and then hit the button. The explosion was louder than the last one and the debris, including the door, went flying past.

Raider waited another second for the dust to settle and then came around the corner. Denlo was already striding into the safety deposit box room. Baker and Wells were also inside.

Raider glanced at Piper. "Might be a good time to split and let the team handle this." He murmured.

She shook her head. "John was clear. I have to see the thumb drive first." She stepped into the room and Raider followed her. None of this was making him feel any better about this mess but hopefully, it would all be over soon.

The thirty-by-thirty room felt even smaller

with all five of them inside. Boxes lined all four walls. Like post office boxes only without a little window on the door. A marble-topped island sat square in the middle of the room so people could set the boxes on it when they were in there. Only a few of the containers had sustained any damage, and it didn't appear like there was anything of any value inside them. Just some paperwork on the floor among the wood and debris.

Denlo was searched for something. He came to a stop in front of a particular set of boxes. "Number two-eighty-three." He tapped it. "I need this opened," he said as he turned to look at Baker and Wells.

They looked at each other and then Baker said, "Let me get the drill." He was back a few moments later, drill in hand.

Wells stepped out of the way and started looking around the room. He went to the boxes that were damaged and started digging around in them. He frowned. "There's nothing here," he said quietly to Raider who was standing next to the hole in the wall. The drill was aloud and masked the sound of his voice. Raider had to lean in slightly to hear it. "I mean all this shit and there's nothing here. I don't get it. Denlo doesn't even really seem upset about the vault." Wells searched Raider's face. "What the hell is going on?"

Raider shrugged silently. There was nothing he could say that was going to stop Wells from connecting the dots at this point. Wells stared at Baker working on the box. Then he turned back to Raider. "He's been after what's in the box all along, right? He just thought the boxes were in the vault."

Again, Raider stayed silent.

"He was going to kill us, wasn't he? I mean once he got whatever he wants from the box. The story about all the cash in the vault was bogus, right? He was going to get what he came for and kill the rest of us."

Raider leaned in slightly. "Just stay calm. This will all be over shortly. Then you and Baker get the hell out of here as fast as you can, okay?"

Wells stared at him, but he remained quiet.

The drilling stopped and Baker opened the small door. Denlo muscled him aside and pulled out the long, flat box and then took it over to the island. He put it down and pointed to the lock. It took Baker no time at all to drill the lock and Denlo threw the lid open.

Craning his neck, Raider could see a thumb drive inside. Denlo grinned. It was the first time since this thing started that Denlo had anything other than a scowl on his face. He reached in and took the thumb drive and tucked it in his pocket.

Then he pulled out his phone and sent off a quick text.

"Okay, we're done," he said and started towards the door. "Everyone out." He motioned with the gun. Wells stared at Baker, who frowned, but both men headed toward the hole in the wall. Raider grabbed Piper by the arm and positioned her so he was between the gun and her. They all trucked down the ladder and climbed back up the stairs into the empty store.

Raider grimaced. If he'd been running the op, then he would've had guys in the bank and here to grab Denlo when he was the last guy to get on to the ladder. Could have easily stopped him from shooting anyone then. Where the hell was the ATF team?

Piper glanced at Raider. He knew she was wondering the same thing. Suddenly the door opened behind them. Raider whirled around. *Finally*. But instead of Chambers and the ATF, it was the clerk from the convenience store. He had a gun in his hand.

The man moved forward so he was lit by the construction lights Baker had set up earlier. His hair was tied back in a ponytail and he wore a dirty pair of jeans. His short-sleeved t-shirt revealed the snake tattoo on his arm.

13

All the air rushed out of Piper's lungs. The convenience store clerk was the Snake. She'd know that tattoo anywhere. All this time he'd been right there. Of course, a tattoo wouldn't be enough. No one would believe that she could ID him by just his tattoo. She'd need more. But he was here and now she knew what he looked like. God she'd kill for a cell phone camera right now.

"You've got it?"

Denlo produced the thumb drive and then immediately tucked it back in his pocket. "What do you want to do?" He indicated Piper, Raider, and the other two with his chin.

"Not here," Snake said. "Too much exposure. Back to the house."

"Hey," Baker said, glancing at Piper and Raider, "I don't want to go back to the house. I want my money and I want off this god-forsaken island. Paradise? Bah!"

Snake raised his gun and pointed it at Baker. "Get in the van or I will shoot you right here." The menace in his tone was unmistakable. He meant business.

Baker raised his hands and stared.

"Now," Snake growled.

Baker and Wells started toward the door. Piper glanced at Raider. This wasn't going according to plan. Not at all. If they got in the van and went back to the house, the chances of surviving this went down dramatically. Where the hell was her backup?

Baker opened the back door and after tossing a glance over his shoulder at Piper, started out. Wells did the same thing. Piper was next through the door. She searched the darkness for any sign of her back-up. Nothing stirred, and the ash in the air blotted out any light, so nothing was visible. Maybe they were in the van? Baker opened the back door, and Piper's heart sank to see the vehicle was empty. He shot her another look. She gave her head the tiniest shake.

Fuck! What the hell was going on? She glanced at Raider. She tried to ask him with her eyes. *Should we get in the van?*

He met her gaze with one eyebrow slightly lifted. *Good question. I have no idea what's going on.*

Piper looked around again. Nothing. Denlo might be an amateur, but the Snake was not. He stood back a bit and held his gun so that he covered their every move. If she or Raider tried anything now, she had no doubt Snake would shoot. She looked at Denlo. He was close but not close enough to grab. *Shit.* They didn't have a choice. They were going to have to get in the van.

She reluctantly climbed in, relieved just a bit when Raider jostled his way into the van after her. His presence and him sticking close to her side was meager relief, but it was a relief. Denlo slammed the door behind them and then climbed around to the driver's seat. The Snake got in on the passenger side. They started driving out when suddenly there were flashing red and blue lights reflected on the van's roof. She looked at Raider who just shook his head. Was this part of their rescue? But Denlo just continued out of the lot and into the street. No one stopped him. Her heart sank.

Piper sat by the back doors of the van between Baker and Wells. Raider was against the wall next to Wells. Baker leaned over and whispered, "I thought they were supposed to come get us."

Snake whirled around and pointed the gun at them. "No talking." He stayed positioned to look back at them so any further conversation was impossible. The truth was she had nothing to say.

She had no clue what had happened. Where was everyone? They should've been there. Then it hit her. They'd finished way early. Like hours early. She glanced at her watch. It was just past one in the morning. They were supposed to be in there for another four hours. Her heart slammed into her rib cage as her stomach lurched.

She tried to suck oxygen into her lungs. At the very least, the ATF should have a spotter on site already. Someone had to be watching the place. Surely the alarm went up when the Snake arrived on the scene. They'd missed him arriving in the warehouse though and it had cost Marta her life. At least when they all came out early, someone would have seen that. She crossed her fingers that the team was probably setting up at the house.

Her nerves settled slightly with the thought. She tried to catch Raider's eye, but it was dark in the back of the van and he seemed to be avoiding looking at her. He was paying more attention to the Snake. Denlo took a corner a bit fast and they all slid into one another.

"Be careful," Snake snarled. "We don't want to attract any attention."

"From who?" Denlo snapped back. "We're the only assholes left here. The lava is still flowing and it's going to cut off the highway. Everyone is gone."

"Don't be stupid."

"Don't fucking tell me what to do, Kasinski."

Kasinski. Now she had a name for him. And she had a face. He was hers. This was all she needed to get justice for Marta.

They pulled up the driveway of the house and Kasinski had them out in the driveway and then into the house in seconds. Piper had been ready for anything when the door of the van opened but nothing happened. She'd been alert when they'd entered the house, but no one was there.

What the fuck was going on?

Her heart rate accelerated, making it difficult to catch a breath. Was help not coming?

Raider stopped in the middle of the great room and turned around. He looked at her and she gave a tiny shake of her head. Wells and Baker both looked at her as well. She didn't know what to tell them. She had no answers and that was terrifying.

"If you're looking at her to find out where the guys are who are going to swoop in and arrest us, then I'm afraid you're out of luck." Kasinski grinned. "No one is coming."

Piper's knees damn near gave out at his statement. She was trying to remain calm, but adrenaline hit her bloodstream like a wave and she was having a hard time keeping her hands from shaking.

"Yeah, we know all about little Miss ATF. Why

the hell did you think you were here? A driver? We didn't need a driver." He stared at her. "But we do need you dead. You could identify me and we can't have that."

"Who is it?" Raider asked.

Kasinski turned the gun on him. "Wouldn't you like to know?"

"Who's what?" Baker demanded. "What in the hell is going on?"

Piper kept her gaze on Kasinski. "Who is the crooked ATF agent? The only way any of this works is if someone with power is crooked. Someone who calls the shots. Fielding. It's got to be Fielding. He was at the warehouse which wouldn't be his normal routine and he's here. Also not normal. You work for Fielding."

Kasinski's smile bordered on demonic. "Never mind who I work for."

Denlo frowned. "Let's just shoot them now and go."

Wells's eyes grew large. He looked at Baker and the two of them backed up.

"Stop moving!" Denlo bellowed. His face was deep red and it wasn't from sunburn. "I'm done with these idiots." He straightened his arm to shoot but Kasinski held up a hand.

"We can't shoot them just yet. He hasn't called." Kasinski quickly checked his phone. "We can't do anything until he calls."

"Why? Just shoot them and be done with this. I'm tired of this shit and my stomach is killing me. I had to eat gluten and I'm in pain."

Kasinski laughed. "I don't give a fuck about your eating habits. We kill them when he says. That's how it works. Tie them up. There's rope in the van."

Denlo cursed a blue streak as he stormed outside toward the van.

Piper glanced at Raider. Any ideas he might have had, he was keeping to himself. They needed a way out. A plan. She couldn't seem to focus though. The idea that Fielding was dirty was too mind-blowing. She took a few deep breaths and tried to center herself.

Denlo was back but he had no rope, only duct tape. "The rope is back at the bank."

Kasinski shook his head. "Whatever."

Denlo made them all sit down and tried to tape Baker's wrists together behind his back but it was impossible. He just couldn't get his wrists close enough to tape them. "Fucking fat pig," Denlo growled.

He taped them together in front of Baker and then taped his ankles. He taped Wells' hands behind his back and did his ankles as well. He had the two men lined up by the sofa.

"You," he said pointing at Piper. "You sit here in the middle of the room."

She did as she was told. Kasinski said nothing but he looked puzzled. When he caught her looking at him, he switched to looking bored.

"You," he pointed at Raider. "Sit with your back to her."

Raider did as he was told and then Denlo taped their hands together in one big mess. Then he taped their legs as well. He stood up and threw the tape across the room. "I'm going to the can," he snarled as he stomped off.

Kasinski stashed his gun in his waistband. "If anyone starts talking, I'll come in and tape your mouths shut." He walked back to the kitchen out of sight.

Piper struggled against the tape but it was no use. Her wrists had been thoroughly immobilized.

"Raider," she whispered. She and Raider were sideways in the middle of the room allowing her to keep watch on the corner by the kitchen for any signs of Kasinski. "Can you move at all?"

"No," he responded. His voice was so quiet she'd had trouble hearing him.

They sat in silence for what seemed like an eternity. Then the sound of the TV in the kitchen being turned on met her ears. Some sort of sporting event.

"Baker," Raider whispered.

Piper had to crane her neck to see Baker at all.

His eyes were huge and he shook his head. "Shut up, man," he whispered.

"Baker," Raider said again. "Just listen to me. Raise your hands as high as you can and bring them down while pulling them apart. The tape will break."

Baker shook his head. He wasn't having it.

"Baker," Raider called softly, "you're the only one who can do this. It's easy and then we can escape."

Baker turned his head away as if he was a toddler.

"Baker," Wells growled. "I wanna live, dude. You can do this. I would if I could."

The sound of a door opening reached them and everyone fell silent. Denlo walked by and glared at them.

He disappeared into the kitchen. "Anything?" Kasinski must have shaken his head because Denlo commented. "I don't know why we can't just kill them now."

"Because Raider is a Navy SEAL and the boss is worried about what kind of heat that's going to bring down on us. He's tried to get details. It's gonna have to look like some kind of accident."

"Fucking shit. I knew this job sucked balls. A fucking Navy SEAL. For shit's sake."

"Calm down. We're getting it sorted." There was a lot of crashing and banging in the kitchen and then, "Go eat that somewhere else. It stinks," Kasinski growled.

"It's cheese."

"I don't give a fuck what it is, it smells. Go somewhere else." Kasinski roared.

Denlo grumbled as he walked through the great room and down the hall.

They stayed a few minutes in silence and then Wells spoke again. Piper craned her neck to see him but she couldn't he was too far over. She cocked her head to try and better hear what he was saying.

"Baker, you gotta do this, man. I got a kid, I don't want to die."

Baker stayed silent.

Wells tried again. "What about your mom? Who will look after her if you're dead?"

Out of the corner of her eye, Piper saw Baker turn his head. A minute later he said, "What do I have to do?"

Raider instructed, "Move out from the couch."

Baker scooched forward a bit.

"Raise your arms above your head and bring them down hard as if you're gonna slap a hip with each hand."

Baker tried it but it didn't work.

"That's okay. You need to really jerk your

arms apart as you bring your hands down. Do it as hard as you can."

Baker raised his arms above his head again and did as he was told. His hands came apart and slammed into the carpet. Everyone froze. Seconds ticked by but neither Snake nor Denlo came running. Baker started pulling the tape off his ankles.

"Baker," Raider called softly. "Come over here. There's a knife in my left boot."

Baker inched in Raider's direction, but it was taking a long time. Instead, he rolled on his belly and pulled himself over. Piper lost sight of him.

"Good, now pull off my boot." There was silence and then she heard the snick of a blade locking into place. A few seconds later Baker was standing up. He disappeared again and then Wells was standing there. The two of them were whispering.

"We're gonna go. Sorry man but we don't want to be busted. This is whack," Wells said as he started to back away.

Piper's belly rolled. "Guys," she said, "you won't make it past Kasinski and Denlo without us. We're trained for this kind of situation. You aren't."

"I didn't see your training doing much for us any other time," Baker snarled.

There was a loud sound from the kitchen. A chair moving. Baker and Wells froze. They all waited in silence. After a full minute, Wells leaned over to Baker and whispered something. Then they both stared down at her and Raider. "If we cut you loose, you have to let us go and not follow us, okay?"

"Agreed," Raider said.

"Deal," Piper responded.

After a slight hesitation, Baker squatted down. He cut Raider's feet first and then came around and cut Piper's. Then Piper leaned forward so he could reach her hands. He cut them both loose. Raider and Piper were on their feet in seconds. Her legs tingled numbly, but the adrenaline coursing through her helped steady her.

Now came the hard part. How were they going to get out of the house without alerting Denlo and Kasinski? The front door was an option but chances were good Kasinski would hear them and come running. They wouldn't have enough time to get away before he started shooting. And they wouldn't have the van. They'd be on foot with deserted roads and a lava flow between them and safety *Think this through*, she told herself. *Be smart*. She clamped her jaws together to keep her teeth from chattering in reaction to the adrenaline.

Raider drew them all in close. "This is what we're gonna do. We're going down that hallway.

The TV is on the opposite wall from this room so chances are good Kasinski is facing away from the opening. I'll check it out and then wave you all down the hallway. It's dark. Stick to the walls."

"Can't we go out the front door?" Baker asked.

Piper shook her head and explained the issue. Raider grabbed the tape as he went to the far wall and checked on Kasinski. He waved Wells down the hallway. Wells disappeared and then he did the same for Baker. Piper joined him against the wall and they went together. A sound reached them all as they were lining the walls. Denlo was returning. Piper's stomach dropped. Raider pointed at the bedroom next to Baker and Wells and they disappeared inside in the darkness. Piper backed into the bedroom they'd stayed in, and Raider followed her but stayed by the door.

Denlo opened the bedroom door and came down the hallway. Before she could blink Raider went out behind Denlo and grabbed him, pulling him inside the room. He had him in a chokehold. It seemed to take forever for Denlo to pass out but once he was out, Piper swung the door closed and they taped up Denlo's hands behind his back and his legs and then put tape over his mouth.

"Get the thumb drive," she demanded. There was no way she was putting her hand in Denlo's pocket. Raider grinned and dug it out and then tucked it in his own pocket. He opened the door and waved for her to precede him down the hallway to the primary bedroom. Baker and Wells followed. Raider closed the door and then walked over to the sliding glass doors.

Piper looked at Baker and Wells. "Okay, guys, we're all gonna go out that door into the woods. You guys stick to the woods as long as you can but head down toward the main street. Baker, I assume you know how to hotwire a car?"

He hesitated and then nodded.

"Good. Steal one of the cars in the neighborhood and drive yourselves to the airport. Get on the next flight out. I never want to see either one of you again. Deal?"

Both men nodded.

"Remember, stick to the woods, and move quickly. If you're on the street, chances are good they'll see you when they come looking."

"Okay," Wells said. "Where are you going?"

"We're gonna do the same thing," she assured them.

Wells nodded again.

Raider opened the door. "Go left. Stick to the wall until you reach the end of the house and then run for the woods."

Wells went first and Baker followed. They did what they were told and made the tree line.

Piper glanced around the room. On the

corner of the desk was a laptop. She grabbed it. She dug around in the closet until she found a backpack and stuck the laptop inside. "In case we get a chance to check out the thumb drive." She stepped out onto the deck and made to follow Wells and Baker. Before she could move, Raider grabbed her hand and then pointed in a slightly different direction. She nodded and the two of them took off for the tree line.

Piper's heart was hammering and sweat was running down her back but they made the tree line but kept running up the hill behind the house. Raider kept up the pace at a good clip.

Piper finally tagged him and asked for a break. "Why are we running uphill?" she asked as she sucked in as much oxygen as she could manage. Kilauea was still spewing ash and making it harder than normal to breathe.

"Because when Kasinski finds us gone, he and Denlo are going to head downhill. That's what makes the most sense."

Piper stared at him gasping. "Do you think they'll find Baker and Wells?"

Raider shrugged. "I hope not, but there's always a chance."

No sooner had the words come out of his mouth than the sound of gunshots reached them.

"Shit," Piper said as she bit her lip. She hoped Wells and Baker were okay.

169

Raider grabbed her hand. "We've gotta move." He pulled the pack off her back and put it on his own.

Piper started running behind him through the trees. How the hell had it come to this? Fucking Fielding. She'd see that man behind bars. If she lived long enough.

14

*R*aider cocked his head and listened to the silence. It didn't make sense to take chances, so he kept Piper moving. His goal was to put as much distance between them and Kasinski and Denlo as possible. According to the map in his head, they were in the Pu'U Maka' Ala Natural Area Reserve. He had no idea if there were any cabins or anything, but he was counting on finding someplace to hunker down.

An hour later, clouds had moved in and between those and the ash filling the sky, they no longer had even a hint of light. Navigating a run through the trees was already hard enough and when it started to rain, he had no choice except to slow their pace to a walk. Raider brought out his cell and used the screen to light a path for a bit.

He didn't want to do it for long because he wanted to conserve the battery, but it was hard to move in the pitch dark in the rain forest. They'd been following a game trail and suddenly they came to a clearing. A small ramshackle cabin sat on one side.

Raider motioned for Piper to wait while he did a three-sixty circuit around it and then hurried back to her side. "It's empty, but I'll go in first. Wait here." Relief filled him when she nodded. Apparently, she'd taken to heart his request to do as he instructed, when he instructed.

She remained hidden among the trees while he approached carefully. He looked in the windows and then picked the lock hanging from a hasp on the door. He waved her over.

The cabin was a one-room affair with a cot in the far corner. There was a small table in front of a stove. There didn't appear to be any running water.

"At least we're not getting rained on anymore," Piper said as she sat down at the table. The rain pinged on the tin roof of the shack, sounding like tiny hammers striking metal.

Raider took off the backpack and took out the laptop. He dried the exterior on a bit of his shirt that wasn't too soaked, then booted it up. "Crap, it's password protected."

Piper rubbed her face. "Well, that sucks."

Raider pulled out his cell and made a call. "Waylen, I need your help."

"Dude, are you okay? Been hearing you're with your ex. Never a good thing."

"You heard right," Raider said but didn't elaborate.

Waylen wasn't wrong. All this time with Piper hadn't been good for him, but he'd stuck to her side like they were still married. He'd deal with the fallout later. "I have a laptop that I need to use and it's password protected."

"I can help," Waylen agreed. "Where are you?"

"In a cabin, I think in the middle of the Pu'U Maka' Ala Natural Area Reserve."

Waylen snorted. "All hell's breaking loose and you're sightseeing. Typical Raider, just typical."

"Funny. How do I get into the laptop?"

Waylen spent the next ten minutes explaining how to get in. Raider executed each step exactly as Waylen directed.

"Yes," Raider said when the desktop appeared on the screen. He inserted the thumb drive. Then double-clicked on the icon for the USB stick when it appeared on the screen. "Shit," he mumbled.

"What?" Waylen demanded.

"It says it's encrypted. Any idea how to break it?"

Waylen's laugh was curt and sardonic. "Sure,

no problem, why don't I solve world hunger while I'm at it? You're in the middle of a freakin' rainforest with no internet. No, I can't break it."

"Just thought I'd ask."

"Do you need to be picked up?" Waylen asked.

Raider leaned back in the chair and glanced at Piper. She looked spent. And soaked. And so damn sexy. "Yeah. I'm guessing it won't happen tonight though."

"Probably not. We can meet you at first light. It's oh-three-thirty. Where do you want to meet and what time?"

Raider snorted. "We're working our way back towards Hilo. We've kind of done a big circle. I'll call you when we get somewhere that has a landmark."

"Okay, brother. Call if you need us to come rescue your ass before that. We'll figure it out."

"Will do." Raider hung up the phone.

He captured Piper's gaze. "Looks like we're here until daybreak. We'll share the cot." He'd been about to offer it to her but fuck that. He'd been through too much today to try sleeping sitting up. He wasn't worried about Kasinski or Chambers finding them tonight, especially since it was raining. The cot wasn't much but it was better than nothing, certainly better than laying down on the grody, dust-covered floor.

Piper opened her mouth to say something but she changed her mind. Instead, she got up and went over to the cot. She lay down on her side facing the wall.

So that's how it was going to be? All the anger that he'd been fighting since he first saw her again came flooding back. She'd kicked him out and now she was going to face the wall like *he* was some kind of monster. He ground his teeth as he lay down next to her. He flipped on his side and faced the door. His ass kissed hers, thanks to the narrow confines of the cot.

Twenty minutes later, he knew he wasn't going to be able to spend the night like this. He was too close to her and not being able to touch her was driving him crazy. Maybe he should sleep in the chair. He might actually get some sleep then. He shifted to his back at the same moment she rolled over and she rolled into his chest. Their gazes locked in the darkness, and he threw caution to the wind and captured her mouth with his. She didn't hesitate but kissed him back with a ferocity that only drove his need higher.

He flipped her on her back and pinned her to the cot with his body. Planting little bites along the side of her neck, he pushed the stray hair out of the way, then lifted her shirt and kissed his way down her chest. He licked the hollow between her breasts, then freed the plump orbs from her bra, eliciting a moan from her as she clutched his t-shirt. With one hand, he jerked it over his head and dropped it to the floor before lowering himself onto her once again. One thigh was tucked between hers, and the heat of her core seared his leg.

She ran her hands over his chest and along his arms and back. She'd always loved his tattoos. Said they were so damn sexy. She ran her hands down to his belt. She started to undo it.

"Slow down," he whispered in between bites. "I need to hear you say you're mine first." He mouthed her nipple again and then grabbed her wrists and held her hands above her head. "Say it, Piper." He licked the sensitive peak of her nipple. "I'm yours, Raider. I want to hear that from you."

His lips found hers again in a heated kiss while she struggled against his grip. He wasn't hurting her, but he wasn't letting go either. He kissed and nipped along her jaw, then down the front of her throat, his tongue dancing in the hollow at the base. As soon as his lips brushed over one of her nipples, she moaned in pleasure.

"God, that's so good," she whispered into his ear. "I've miss this so much, missed you so much."

He pulled back and held her gaze. He shifted until both his legs were between her thighs and his hips nestled against her center. The words were uttered in a soft voice but there was no mistaking he was serious. "Say it, Piper. Say you're mine. We both know it's true. Just say it."

He needed her to admit she still wanted him as much as he wanted her. The idea that she'd been with any other man was enough to drive him insane. He needed to hear her say she was his. Always had been. Always would be. Just as he was hers. Forever.

He rocked his hips hard against her center. Taking control of the kiss once again, he used his tongue to leave her breathless. He moved slowly from her lips to kiss a trail down her neck and then to each of her nipples, tugging lightly at them until she gasped for air. "Say it." She struggled against his hold, but he maintained a tight grip. He lifted off her body, withdrawing the heat he was certain she was craving. He lowered his head and whispered in her ear, "Say it, Piper. Or I'll stop."

She yelped when he groaned and playfully nipped at her breast. He was still holding himself off her, and she was certain he'd make good on his promise to stop. He'd always had amazing control during sex. Loving her to the brink, then easing her back to earth and starting all over again. The number of times she could orgasm before him was astounding. And oh, so good.

Raider rolled her onto her stomach on the cot and held her hands above her head as he alternated kisses and bites down her neck and her back. His cock pressed against the curve of her backside, and it only added to the intense heat coursing through her body. She was wet and ready and he hadn't even taken off her pants yet. She'd missed this man. Her husband. She'd missed his touch so damn much. A moan escaped her lips.

Moving his hand around to the front, he found the apex of her legs and began massaging her through the fabric of her jeans.

"Take them off," she whispered, lifting her hips upward.

Raider quickly undid the button and zipper, pulling the jeans down her legs. As he kissed her neck, his fingers slipped inside the edge of her thong. He gently rubbed her clit, teasingly slow as she squirmed under him. Her anticipation grew until she couldn't take it anymore.

"Faster," she pleaded.

He rose to his knees behind her and removed his fingers from her thong. She whimpered, but he was relentless. "Say it, Piper" he whispered. "I won't let you come until you say it. You're mine."

Un-fucking-believable. She bit her lip and shook her head. If she said it now, it would be real, and she feared the possibility of real with Raider. What the hell had the last five years been about? While she struggled with the questions and uncertainty, he sighed behind her. The tiniest whisper of air on her spine.

He went back to teasing her clit. Beneath him, she writhed with pleasure until he finally pushed his fingers deep inside of her, earning a loud moan from her lips.

Turning her over once again, he removed her underwear. He kissed her belly, and the tender gesture made every nerve in her body beg for him.

Pressing his body tightly against hers, Raider kissed her deeply. The feeling of their bare skin touching ignited an intense desire, one Piper had thought she would never experience again. As his fingers explored between her legs once more, she moved erratically beneath him. With each touch to her sensitive center, she found herself falling further into ecstasy. Raider made his way down her body until he was kneeling above the apex of her legs, ready to give her the thing she craved; his hot breath against her skin. As he caressed the heated folds at the apex of her thighs, she eagerly responded to his skilled touch. With deliberate movements, he blew a cool breath over her core as she sunk her fingers into his hair and held his head to her core.

His hands bit into her hips, keeping her in place as he used his tongue on her clit. She moaned and he intensified the lashings of his tongue. She locked her legs around his head and let go of his hair, gripping the sides of the cot as she tried to fight the waves of desire burning through her. Then he inserted a finger inside while continuing to pleasure her with his mouth. He picked up speed and added another finger.

Piper pushed against his fingers and bit her lip to hold back her scream. She was on the brink, and she wanted him so badly she actually ached with need.

Raider, her Raider. This was heaven, one she never thought she'd see again. He pushed a third finger inside her. She lifted her hips to meet him, reaching the peak of ecstasy. With a sudden nip of his teeth against her most sensitive spot, she cried out his name and climaxed.

Without giving her a break, he spread himself on top of her and started sucking on her nipples. His cock pounded with the need to be inside her, to feel her sweet, wet heat surround him. To know he owned her. At the same time, he wanted to punish her for kicking him out. Punish her for not being able to be with her, for not having this delicious heaven in his life. With a growl, he slammed his cock inside her, making her entire body shudder. She cried out, the sound muffled by his lips as he claimed her with a searing kiss. His hands gripped her hips, pulling her closer, driving deeper.

Piper writhed beneath him, her body responding to his every touch. Her moans rose above the sound of the rain on the roof each time he thrust into her. The pounding rhythm he set kept time with the pounding of his heart.

The intensity between them was familiar and insane. The raw desire he had for her was like nothing else and it only fueled his passion more. This was what he craved for five long years and now he was going to take it again and again.

He continued to thrust, his hips moving in a frenzied dance, his breath ragged and heavy. She clung to him, her body arching towards his, pulling his hair, digging her nails into his shoulders. A sharp sting hit his pec. She'd bit him, and the act only made him want her more. His hips thrust harder, and their bodies moved in a feverish rhythm fueled by need and anger.

And love. He'd never fallen out of love with her. The knowledge made him drive harder, deeper. Joining them in the most primal way.

This was a battle of desire and will, where they'd both win.

Raider's eyes snagged her gaze. "Tell me you're mine," he demanded.

Eyes hazed, she clawed at his back, her nails digging into his skin, and he met her intensity with his own.

"I'm yours, Raider. I always have been." The words tumbled from her lips, one final surrender to the raw desire that had consumed them both.

Raider's heart thumped triumphantly, his breath ragged and heavy. He thrust into her, their bodies moving in perfect synchrony, their hearts pounding in rhythm, Piper's gaze locked on his. With a growl, he thrust deeper, his body trembling with desire.

"Say it again," he grunted, his voice low and gritty.

"I'm yours, Raider," she whispered. "And you're mine."

Oh God, he'd happily be hers if he could have her like this every night. Raider plunged into her one final time, burying himself deep within her as the world around them disappeared into a whirl of sensations. Beneath him, her body convulsed, her moans filling the small cabin as she reached the pinnacle. Raider's orgasm was imminent, A tingling building at the base of his spine, raging within him like an inferno ignited by her surrender and the intensity of their connection.

As he climaxed, his eyes never left hers, his intensity unwavering. "You're mine," he growled, his voice low and rough. He added silently *and you always will be*.

15

*P*iper swung her legs over the edge of the cot. Being curled up with Raider had been heaven but now it was time to move on. Time to take care of her. The sex had been as masterful as it always had been, but it was also almost her undoing. Raider owned her body. He always had and she was powerless to escape him when he was close.

To put distance between them, she got up, took the phone off the table, and then stepped outside the cabin. It would start to be light soon. They needed to move but first, she needed to make a call.

She dialed the number. "Hey," she said when the call was answered.

"Piper?" John Chambers' voice came down the line. "Is that you?"

"Yeah."

"Where the hell are you? What happened? Are you in the bank? We're not seeing any movement. You guys should be out by now."

Piper was leery of saying too much. On one hand, John was her boss and had always had her back, but on the other hand, she had questions. "We left a while ago. Why was there no spotter? Why didn't you have eyes on the bank?"

"We did," John protested. "We didn't see anything. The guy I had watching had to back off some cops from coming into the strip mall but that was the only time he left his post."

They'd seen the flashing lights when they were leaving. Could it really just have been bad timing? "Where's Fielding?"

"Why? You want to talk to him? He's back at the office."

She took a deep breath. "John, I think he's dirty." There was a long silence on the other end of the phone. "They knew," Piper continued, "Denlo and Snake knew I was ATF. Hell, they admitted, almost bragged that they had a guy on the inside. It has to be Fielding. He showed up at the warehouse bust unexpectedly, when Marta died"—her voice cracked but she hurried on— "and he showed up here. Neither of those situations warranted him being around."

"I...don't know, Piper. Fielding is a pretty big

deal. It would be insane if he were dirty. He has access to everything."

She ran a hand over her face. "I know but the fact that we know so little about this organization, doesn't that scream inside man?"

"I…guess."

"Look, John. All I'm saying is keep your eye on Fielding."

"Fine. I'll see what I can do but first, we need to bring you in. Where are you?"

She laughed. "Good question. Somewhere in one of the rainforest reserves. Raider will get us out. As soon as we hit civilization, we'll call."

"Okay. Piper, do you have the thumb drive?"

She started to answer when she heard a sound in the darkness. "Gotta go." She hung up and went back inside the cabin. Raider was standing in the middle of the room stretching.

"Did you call Chambers?"

"Yeah, I'll call him again when we're out of here. There was rustling in the forest. Do you think they found us?"

Raider shook his head. "Kasinski doesn't strike me as the nature type and neither does Denlo. They didn't track us especially after it started raining. Remember the gunshot? I'm pretty sure they followed Wells and Baker. What you heard was probably just an animal." He was being deliberately cool and professional. Not showing her any warmth and not meeting her gaze for any length of time.

She couldn't blame him. They'd had amazing sex but that didn't change anything. She'd still kicked him out without giving him the real reason. He didn't trust her. Smart man. Giving in to lust didn't change the past and it couldn't alter their future.

"It's starting to get light. We should go."

Raider nodded. "You stay here. I'll have a look around and then we'll go." He quietly shut the cabin's door as he left.

"Okay." Piper sat at the table for a moment and tried to pull herself together. It had been days since she'd had a shower, and her clothes were a mess. She was a mess. The rain had helped a bit in terms of washing some of the dirt off, but her hair was a disaster. She wrapped her hair in a bun and put the elastic back around it. She must look a fright, not that it mattered.

She closed her eyes and ran her hands over her face. This whole situation was tough, made tougher by spending so much time with Raider. It sucked that she still loved him so damn much. Sleeping with him had been heaven. Being safe in his arms with the world at bay was a balm to her jangling nerves, one that she missed with a ferocity that scared her.

Piper dragged herself to her feet. Raider

wasn't hers anymore no matter how much she loved him. She'd made a choice five years ago, an impetuous choice she'd made during a weapons bust, not even really thinking about it, and her world had changed because of it. One tiny decision had cost her everything. For five long years, she'd lived with the consequences and one of those was losing Raider. Taking a deep breath, she straightened her shoulders and then opened the door. She just had to get through this next bit and then she could fall apart.

Raider was at the edge of the clearing, waiting for her. Silently, she handed him the backpack and fell into step behind him.

The pace Raider had set was fast, but the trek wasn't too taxing. Three hours later they emerged from the rain forest into a flat, grassy area alongside a dirt road. The sun was above the horizon and the day was heating up. Raider pulled out his cell and made a quick call to Harlan to let him know that Raider and Piper were out of the forest on a dirt road somewhere by Hilo.

"No problem. We'll find you."

Raider hung up and handed Piper the phone. She called John and told him the same thing. Then she clicked off the call. She wasn't keen to talk to anyone. They had walked in silence the entire time. Now her time with Raider was coming to an end.

She was trying to decide if she should tell him now or wait until after everyone came when Raider made the decision for her.

"Once the world gets here we won't have time to talk. When this is sorted, I don't want to meet up again. It's too damn hard. So, I kept my end of the deal. Now keep yours. Why did you kick me out? And don't tell me it was because I was gone too much."

Piper took a deep breath and blew out. "No, that wasn't it." Suddenly her throat closed over and she just couldn't get the words out. The truth was just too crushing. It could destroy this man she still loved so, so much.

She swallowed convulsively a few times and then finally she managed to utter an apology. "I'm sorry." Those words seemed to release the dam she'd built inside herself because it all came out in a torrent then.

"What I did was completely unfair but I...I didn't want you to hate me." She shook her head. "No, that's not true. You hate me anyway. I didn't have the nerve to tell you the truth that I knew would make you hate me on a fundamental level. Not just *hey we don't get along anymore, my ex is a bitch*, but more of the *I wish my ex-wife didn't exist* kind of thing."

Raider stared at her. "What are you talking about?"

"You were… wherever you were… and I was working a case. It was a weapons thing. We were running a nighttime op by the docks. It was dark, so damn dark, Raider. There was no moon and a light breeze." She paused. "Funny how those details stick in your mind." She remembered exactly how the shadows fell on the pier. She remembered the cold chain link biting into her fingers.

"What happened?" Raider prompted. He looked mystified how any of this could have anything to do with her kicking him out.

Wait. Just wait. She cleared her throat. "The deal went down as expected. The seller had the guns. Our team posed as buyers flush with cash. As soon as the exchange happened, we swarmed in to make the arrests." She took another breath.

"The head seller had hung back slightly. He saw us coming and did a runner. I gave chase. John yelled at me to wait for backup… but I couldn't. The guy would've gotten away, so I went." She paused, fearful of reliving all the details. But she owed Raider the truth. She hauled in a deep breath and continued. "He went out onto the dock and ran back towards the street. He was fast but I was gaining on him. Then he suddenly disappeared into one of the shadows on the dock. I slowed down and cleared the area. I

should've waited like John said but… I didn't."
Regret choked her again.

Raider didn't even lay a hand on her arm to offer comfort. Not that she'd have tolerated the gesture. If he was too kind, she'd never get this out.

"A few minutes later, he burst from the shadows and made a run for the chain link fence that separated part of the dock we were on. I went after him. The fence was high and old. He made it over and took off down the street. I wasn't as lucky. I made it to the top and then my foot got caught and I fell to the sidewalk. I hit hard. Hit my head and my shoulder. I passed out."

"When I came to, I was in the hospital. The nurse told me…" Piper swallowed once again. "Told me that I'd lost our baby. I had been eleven weeks pregnant." Her heart splintered in her chest once more. It had shattered into little pieces that day and since then, she'd worked to mend it. Now the hairline cracks were splitting wide open.

Raider stopped walking and stared at her. "Did you know?" his voice broke on the last word. His eyes were wide and his face had lost color.

She tried to speak but her voice was gone. She was crushing him all over again and it had stolen her breath, her voice, and her soul. She just nodded. Driving her fingernails into her other hand helped clear the lump of tears from her throat so she could speak. "I didn't tell you. I wanted to surprise you when you came home. I knew how much you wanted children. How much you wanted a child with me." She shook her head. "I didn't even think of the baby, of our child, when I took off after the runner. The pregnancy never even crossed my mind until I was falling off the fence."

Raider stared at her, his hands opening and closing. He wanted to kill her and she didn't blame him. She'd gone through that stage herself. Along with all the other stages of grief. "Raider, I just couldn't face you. I couldn't tell you the truth and have you hate me for…" her voice broke. "For killing our child."

The sound of tires crunching on gravel hit her ears. She glanced in the direction of the sound to see an SUV and another car coming up the road. The cavalry had arrived. Too bad they couldn't save her from the torture she'd endure for the rest of her life. From seeing the pain and anguish on Raider's face.

16

*R*aider could barely breathe let alone focus on what was happening around him. Piper had been pregnant. *Pregnant.* He'd always wanted a family. A large one. Piper said yes to two with a possibility of three, but Raider had wanted six. He'd given up on that ever happening once she'd kicked him out. Just the thought that it had been a reality at least for a little while and she hadn't told him. The idea of all they'd lost, all he'd lost demolished something in him. He wanted to shake her. What the hell had she been thinking? Why didn't she tell him? She'd wanted it to be a surprise. Well, she got her wish. Even five years later, it was a hell of a surprise.

The vehicles had come to a halt and Chambers had gotten out of the car and was walking towards them. "Piper, I'm so glad you're okay. You gave us a hell of a scare. What a clusterfuck last night was! So glad it all worked out."

"Yeah, me too," Piper said.

Her voice was strained, and she was pale. There was no way Chambers wouldn't know something was wrong. Raider's first instinct was still to protect her from anything, including her boss's potential prying.

He gave himself a mental shake. He needed to let her go. She'd made it clear she was done with him. She'd had five years to process the loss of their child. He'd had five minutes. *She should be worried about him!* Instead, she was just quiet and pale. This whole thing was like getting hit by shrapnel. Emotional shrapnel that was going to leave permanent damage.

Chambers gaze darted back and forth between the two of them. "Do you have the thumb drive?"

Raider studied Chambers. He was sweating and he looked like he hadn't slept in days. *Know the feeling.* Raider wasn't sure he'd ever sleep again after Piper's bombshell. He frowned. He needed to get through this and get away. He needed time to process…his loss. Both of them.

"Did Baker and Wells make it?" Piper asked suddenly. "We heard gunshots. I was worried."

"Er, not sure. Haven't seen them. Don't know

anything about it. We can send a team to the neighborhood to look."

Faint alarm bells were ringing for Raider, but he'd be damned if he could put his finger on why. He glanced toward the other vehicle behind Chambers' car. No one had gotten out of it. He jammed his hands in his pockets and touched a button on the cell phone. A little insurance just in case.

"Who's in the SUV?" he asked.

Chambers glanced over his shoulder. "No one, just some team members. I brought them along but since there's no issue they're probably staying in the A/C."

Raider nodded but his gut told him something was way off. The passenger window was down in the SUV, but he couldn't see inside. Whoever sat there wasn't worried about staying cool. "Where's Fielding?"

"Like I told Piper, he's back at the office. He's waiting to hear about the thumb drive. You have it, right Piper?"

She nodded. "Yeah, we have it."

"Great. You can just give it to me and then we'll get you back to the office and debrief you." Chambers was really sweating now. It was not warm enough to justify that kind of perspiration, even with a suit and tie.

"Did you guys get Denlo and his boss?" Raider asked nonchalantly.

Chambers cleared his throat nervously. "Picked them up at the house. Denlo screamed bloody murder, but Kasinski came quietly."

Icy fingers gripped Raider's heart. He glanced at Piper. Did she pick up on it? He shifted his weight so he'd be ready to move while trying to get her attention without being obvious, but she was oblivious to him.

She was frowning and then she cocked her head. "Wait, how did you know…" her voice died as her eyes widened. "It's you," she said. "You're the mole. You're the one that got Marta killed."

Piper couldn't believe the man she'd called boss and mentor, a man who'd been a friend for years could be the mole. How was that even possible?

But the facts fit.

And if she had any doubts the gun in his hand that was pointed at her was a clear message.

"How could you?" she demanded. Her heart rate skyrocketed, and heat crept into her cheeks. She closed her hands into fists. "Marta is dead because of you. Why?"

John just kind of shrugged. "I needed the money," he said simply. "Pauline took me to the cleaners in the divorce. I can't afford to pay her alimony, pay for the kids, and still live. I got tired of working my ass off for so little." The normally affable animation left her boss's face. All the friendliness was gone. Now he'd morphed into just another cold, calculating killer. His eyes had even gone flat.

Bile rose in her throat. She wanted to puke. "But Marta died!" Piper just couldn't get her brain around it. "You brought Marta into the division. You were her mentor. How could you let Kasinski kill her?" His treachery was unfathomable to her.

"The same way he's going to let me kill you." Kasinski appeared on Piper's right flank. "You are a real pain in the ass. I stomped through the fucking forest all night looking for you. I'll take that thumb drive now." He shoved his hand into her belly.

Instinctively, Piper moved closer to Raider. She wanted to protect him. If this was her moment to go, she was fine with it. but she couldn't deal with it if she got Raider killed. She should have never brought him into this. How crazy did she have to be to endanger him, while she still loved him so much? She shook her head, scattering the damning thoughts. "You killed Marta."

"Yes," John agreed. "That didn't really go

according to plan. You and Marta weren't supposed to be in the warehouse. If you'd both just stayed outside... but no. Both of you were always so impulsive. I should've known better than to have you two there at the buy. That wasn't the way I wanted it to go, but I couldn't think of a way to keep you out of the operation. If anyone is at fault, it was Marta's. She sealed her fate the moment she went into that warehouse."

Pain and anger lanced Piper's brain. *The son of a bitch.*

John raised his gun higher. "And so did you. If you'd just let the whole thing go, it would've been fine. But no. You had to push and push." He made a face and said in a high-pitched voice as if to mimic her, "The man with the snake tattoo. He did it. The Snake, we have to find him." Malice dripped off his words like water off a leaf during a rainstorm.

He dropped his voice to normal. "Honestly, I got so tired of hearing about it. If you'd have let it go, then we wouldn't be here. This job never needed a driver. If you'd just let Marta's death go, then I wouldn't have had Slick reach out and you wouldn't ever have to be here. But you always knew better than anyone. So tenacious, like a fucking pit bull. Your theory was starting to get some interest from the higher-ups, and I couldn't risk that. You never know when to quit. And you have such an over-developed sense of justice. I knew you'd get on the plane. No way you could let the opportunity go by. Hell, if you'd followed the rules then I'd be screwed but no, you had to jump in to find the perp responsible for the death of your colleague." A slow, mean smile lit his face. "How's that working out for you?"

Piper didn't know what to say. She had no idea who the cold-blooded killer in front of her was. Not her boss John. No, it was a total stranger, one she never knew existed.

"Give me the thumb drive," Kasinski said and held out his hand.

Piper once again moved closer to Raider. She was now almost touching him. If nothing else, she might be able to give him a fighting chance. She owed him that after what she'd done. She searched for something to distract them. Maybe with enough time to think, Raider could come up with a plan. "What happened to Denlo? Where's he?" she blurted out.

"Dead," Kasinski said, his voice full of disgust. "That asshole let you get away and then he started to bitch about everything. He was in a panic about you guys escaping. Said the boss was going to kill us if we didn't get the thumb drive back. He was out of control and falling apart so I put him out of his misery."

"The shots," Raider said.

Kasinski smiled. "You should have seen his face when I put the first slug into him. He didn't see it coming. Always the best way if you ask me but Denlo was right about one thing, my life is over if I don't produce that thumb drive." He waved his gun. "I won't ask again."

Piper's heart surged faster and sweat ran down between her shoulder blades. She turned to John. "What are you going to do about us? What will you tell the others? Where does Fielding think you are right now?"

Her boss shrugged slightly. "Fielding is the least of my worries. He never spent much time in the field, so he has no real idea of what goes on. I had the team breach the house at dawn. Once they found it empty, they had to sit around and discuss how to deal with it until forensics showed up. Now I have the backup team out driving around looking for the van along with Denlo and Kasinski. Eventually, they'll find Denlo and the van. It's parked behind someone's house in the same neighborhood. But it might take them a while. Probably not until people are allowed back in. Kilauea has been good to me." His mean smile was back.

"But what will you tell him happened here?" she pushed.

"I'll tell him the truth. Kasinski killed you both and then got away. It happens. It's horrible but it happens. I'll be so broken up about it, I'll have to take some time off. Then I'm gonna head to the Caribbean and get lost. No more alimony payments, no more paying for the kids, just me in the sunshine with a rum drink in my hand." He had a far-off look in his eye as if he was already seeing himself on that beach. Wait, was he humming "Margaritaville"? God, she hoped he stepped on that damn pop top and lost a leg to gangrene.

"Now," he said as he snapped back to the present. "Give us the thumb drive or I'll take it off your cold dead body."

Raider startled her with a snort of laughter. "You already told us you're gonna kill us. Not like you've given us any incentive to hand it over. Once you have it, we're dead anyway."

"Just give me the fucking drive," Chambers snarled.

Piper turned her head slightly. Then she glanced at Raider who met her gaze. He heard it too. She was sure of it. She glanced around. If they could get to the SUV, they could get away. She gave Raider the tiniest of nods. She was on board for whatever he was planning. There wasn't a doubt in her mind that she would do whatever it took to get him out of this alive. He deserved to enjoy his retirement. Enjoy the rest of his life.

Maybe he'd meet someone and have those children he wanted so badly.

She swallowed hard and then stared at her boss. "Come and get it you son of a bitch," she said.

17

*R*aider grabbed Piper's hand and pulled as he dodged between the shots. When he'd heard the *whomp whomp* of the approaching chopper he knew his team was coming for him. He caught a glimpse of Lane and Harlan hanging out of the open door of the chopper, firing their weapons as they flew overhead. Raider pulled Piper along as fast as he could and aimed for the SUV. *Fucking keys had better be in the ignition.*

Suddenly Piper let out a small screech and Raider's arm jerked backward. She was down. His heart skipped a beat, then another. Piper had to be okay. He couldn't lose her like this. She couldn't die. The smile on Kasinski's face was deadly as he fired at them again. Thank fuck his aim was horrendous. Most people didn't have a clue about keeping a weapon steady as they ran. The metallic ping of a bullet hitting the SUV beyond Raider was terrifying. Taking advantage of the brief reprieve, Raider bent and scooped Piper into his arms as the chopper swung around and opened fire, once more providing him cover.

Raider made it to the SUV and put Piper in the passenger seat. He ran around and slid behind the wheel. He hit the button to start it but no dice. He cursed a long time in his head. He'd decided running back toward the tree line was too risky. It was too far, but now that Piper was shot, he was second-guessing his choices.

Kasinski must have the keys and he was running toward them gun raised. Raider hunkered down as bullets burst through the windshield and also went into the engine block. Raider knew there was only one thing for it. "Hang on, Piper," he said as he counted off the seconds and then once Kasinski was close enough, he hit the start button and the SUV roared to life. He threw it in reverse and pulled a K-turn. They were rocketing down the road in seconds.

In the rearview mirror, Kasinski and Chambers were racing toward the other car when Harlan and Lane shot it to pieces. Raider grinned and then glanced at Piper. She was pale and her fingers, where they were pressed to her side, were bright red.

But she was alive, goddammit. "I'm okay," she mumbled. "Just a flesh wound."

He didn't like the look of her so he hit the gas. About two miles down the dirt road, the SUV sputtered and died. "Fuck," he growled. He pulled out his cell phone, but he couldn't get a response from any of his teammates. They'd be in the chopper and not hearing their phones. He dialed nine-one-one and gave details. He asked for police as well as an ambulance. He explained the situation and told them help was needed ASAP.

"Piper, how're you holding up?" He didn't like the gray pallor on her cheeks.

"I'm okay." She offered him a small smile. "How long until help arrives?"

"Could be a while. The dispatcher didn't like to say." And that caused him panic but he wasn't gonna share that with her. It helped that his team had shot the shit out of the other SUV. Hopefully they'd disabled it.

"John and Kasinski aren't that far behind. Maybe we should look for a place to hide," Piper suggested. Her voice was breathy, and her hand was pressed tightly to her side.

Raider glanced out the window. There were fields and a distant tree line. One house was in view but it was quite far off. Even if he got Piper there, it would be the first place that Chambers and Kasinski would look. It was also far from the police and ambulance, if they ever showed up.

"It's better to stay put." He didn't want to jostle Piper too much. "How bad is it?"

"Well, it's not a simple graze,"

"Shit." He had no idea where the bullet was and moving her might do more damage. He opened the center console. Kasinski must have taken Denlo's weapon because there was a Glock inside. "Thank God," he muttered as he checked for ammo. Not a full clip but he had six shots. Good thing Waylen wasn't the only crack shot on the team.

"Do you have a number for Fielding?" Raider asked. Piper didn't respond. "Piper?" he said again. Still nothing. She'd passed out. At least that's what he was telling himself. There was a tremble in his hand as he reached out to check her pulse. Clenching his fist, he sent up a prayer, then flexed his hand, and laid his fingers on her neck, praying for a pulse. It was there, although a bit slow.

He ran a hand through his hair and then glanced over at her. Two things were abundantly clear to him. He was still madly in love with her, and he was royally pissed with her. Like so mad he wanted to spit nails.

She groaned and then her eyelids fluttered open. "Raider?" she said.

"I'm here." He reached over and grabbed her hand.

"How long was I out for?" she blinked slowly.

"Only a few minutes." He alternated looking at her and checking the mirrors for any signs of Chambers and Kasinski. Seeing her like this was twisting his gut into knots when he should be focused on saving their asses. She just had to be okay.

"Raider, I just want to say how sorry I am. I never should've dragged you into this. I never should've gotten on the airplane. I suspected…no, I knew there was something off about the whole thing. I guess I gave in to my impetuous nature one too many times." She shrugged and then grimaced. More crimson blood oozed between her fingers.

To distract her he gave a harsh laugh. "It won't be the last time. It's who you are."

Raider glanced at his watch. They'd been sitting still for ten minutes. Time was running short.

"But I think it might be the last time. I'm thinking of quitting the ATF. I…it's not the same anymore. I…Anyway, I just wanted you to know how sorry I am." She looked right at him. "For everything."

He knew what she was talking about. She was sorry about running after the fucking perp, which caused her to lose their baby. He ground his teeth. He still wasn't ready to talk about it. It was gonna take a while for him to work out all the shit on his mind.

"You'll feel better once you get to a hospital. Don't plan your future just yet." He deliberately ignored what she was saying. Now wasn't the time to deal with the idea of her being pregnant. Nor did he have the capacity to examine his emotions at this point. His job now was to keep them alive.

She stared at him but then just nodded.

He fucking hated sitting in the car on the road. They were too exposed but he didn't see they had a choice. He kept the Glock in his right hand and swiveled his gaze. "Piper, don't pass out on me," he added as he glanced at her.

"I won't. I'm good." She glanced in her side mirror. "Do you think John knows who the head of the arms ring is?"

He grabbed at the question like it was a lifeline. He didn't want to talk about *them* any more than she did. "If I had to guess, I'd say no. The smart money says this ring is pretty compartmentalized. The right hand doesn't even know it has a left hand. One thing they do all know is that the list was out there but no one mentioned a name attached to it. I think whoever is at the top, knows what they're doing. I think this fuck up is on Chambers and Kasinski."

"You don't think it's Fielding on top?" she pushed.

"It would be convenient, but I don't think so. If it was, he wouldn't be anywhere near here. He'd want as much distance as possible between this mess and him. Whoever is running this is smart and keeps a tight ship."

A figure was running up behind them. The way he moved, Raider was pretty sure it was Chambers. "Heads up," he said as he watched in the mirror. Kasinski was nowhere in sight. The sky was gray and dotted with fine bits of ash. He longed to see the chopper with his friends on it, but he had a feeling they were putting it down somewhere. They'd come to check on him but only after he didn't show up in a bit.

"Piper, Chambers is coming. He doesn't have a gun in his hands. I'm going to get out of the SUV and face him. I want you to do me a favor, hunker down in the wheel well as best you can. If this turns into a firefight, you'll have a much better chance down there."

"Raider?" she said, her voice raised in a question.

"Don't worry, honey. I've got this. Just get low."

Piper bit her lip and stared at him. He gave her a nod of encouragement, but she still didn't move. He was watching Chambers get closer and closer.

"Come on, Piper, get down. What I say, when I say it, right? That's what you agreed."

She nodded and then started to move but grunted in pain. "Raider, in case things go badly—"

"It's gonna be fine. Just get on the floor." He was losing his patience.

"Raider," Piper said again, her tone was odd, so he turned to glance at her. "I love you," she declared and then did as she was told.

Raider didn't have time to process those words. He was out of the SUV and standing with the driver's door open behind him facing Chambers. "Stop right there," he said. He didn't bother to raise the gun. He knew he could shoot the other man before he could get his gun out of wherever he'd stashed it.

Chambers crashed to a halt about twenty feet behind the SUV. He raised his hands. "Kasinski is dead," he called.

Raider didn't respond.

"I need your help."

Raider still stayed silent. Whatever this was, it wasn't what it appeared to be.

"Seriously, I need your help." Chambers' face was beet red, and he was sweating profusely. "I have to give my boss the thumb drive or he'll kill me." Chambers holds out his hands. "I didn't have a choice in any of this. I mean, I was stupid and I accepted some money for some information and it all went south from there." Chambers pointed to his own chest. "I tried to get out of it, I did. But they threatened my children."

Raider kept his gaze on a swivel. From the set-up he was pretty sure he knew what Chambers was trying to do. "Who's your boss?" he finally asked playing along.

"What?" Chambers called back.

"Who's your boss?"

Chambers' face went blank and Raider's instincts juddered. Chambers hadn't thought Raider would ask about his boss. Now, the jerk was trying to recover.

"I...I can't tell you. He'd kill me for that, too."

"Then I guess you're gonna die," Raider responded calmly. He was calling Chambers' bluff. If the man told him who his boss was then he thought Raider was going to die. If he maintained the secret then he wasn't confident in his plan.

Chambers growled, "Come on, Raider, you don't know what these people are like. They're stone-cold killers, and they have no problem killing my family."

"I don't really care, Chambers. You can tell me who your boss is and maybe I won't shoot you, or you can keep your secret and die. Either way works for me."

"Asshole," Chambers said in a much quieter voice, but Raider caught it anyway. Chambers shrugged, and Raider knew that he'd decided to share the boss's name which meant he was pretty sure of his plan to get out of there alive."

"Senator Josh Atlee."

Raider vaguely knew who Chambers was talking about. His talk with Lane made him think it would be someone high up. No one has access to military-grade weapons without having some kind of connection. In the end, it didn't really matter. Chambers had told him so now as far as Chambers was concerned, Raider and Piper's death warrant was signed.

"I need that thumb drive," Chambers called.

"You're not going to get it." Raider was done playing.

Chambers' face hardened. "Just give me the fucking drive. You can't open it anyway. It's encrypted."

"*I* may not be able to, but I sure know some people who can and they're going to be very interested in what's on it. I'm guessing Atlee isn't the only politician on the list. I bet there's all kinds of interesting names on it." A sudden thought hit him. "That's what this is all about, isn't it? You were getting the list for yourself. You planned on blackmailing all the other SOBs whose names are on the list."

Chambers' face suffused with color and then it turned pale.

Bull's-eye. Raider snorted. "Where did you think you were going to hide out?"

"Give me what I fucking want right now," Chambers yelled, frustration dripping from every word. He was royally pissed now. His body was vibrating. The man was starting to lose it. Then his head turned slightly to the right and his right hand closed into a fist.

Raider immediately turned to his left and fired through the SUV. He hit Kasinski in the middle of his forehead as he approached Piper's side of the vehicle. Then Raider swung back and aimed at Chambers' forehead.

The other man's eyes widened. He had his hands up for real this time. "Don't shoot me."

"I can't think of one good reason why I shouldn't." This was the man who was responsible for Piper getting shot, for Marta dying, and for all kinds of other shit, he was sure.

"Raider?" Piper's voice reached him. "As much as I want him dead for Marta, I think I'd like him alive and in jail even more."

The sound of vehicles approaching had Raider immediately turning sideways, still pointing the gun at Chambers but watching to see who arrived. Three cars pulled up and Raider immediately recognized Fielding coming out of the second one. Then an ambulance arrived.

Other ATF agents exited the vehicles and swarmed Chambers like ants on a hill. Raider lowered the gun to his side and turned toward Piper. She was sitting in the seat again but looking pale.

"I love you too," he said. And then turned and walked away.

18

---

*P*iper stared out the window. They wanted to keep her in for one more night. She sighed. What she really wanted was to get on an airplane and get the hell out of there. If only she had a clue where to go. Or even where she wanted to go. San Diego was out of the question. Not only had she lost Marta there, but also Raider, and now, in a fucked up way, John. He'd been her mentor, her father-figure since her own father lived in Florida. He'd molded her into the agent she was and now he was in jail.

She admired the view. The trees here were so green and the water was magnificent. Hawaii had a nice feel to it. Maybe she'd move here permanently and...do what? She had time to figure that part out. Her bank account was healthy. She hadn't spent any money in the last five years past food and rent. Rarely going out had its advantages. She could move to Hawaii and live on her savings for at least six months or until a job came along. Hell, she could be a barista in a coffee shop and at least get benefits.

The room door opened and Tom Fielding walked in. She'd been hoping Raider would visit her, even though she knew it was a long shot.

"Assistant Director Fielding," she said, trying to sit up a little straighter but wincing with the effort.

He waved her off as he approached the bed. "Relax. You've been shot. Take all the time you need to heal."

Piper tried not to grimace. Was that his way of telling her she wasn't going back to work? Not that she could blame him but suddenly, even though she'd been thinking about quitting the ATF, the thought of losing her job on top of everything else made her heart hurt. "Thanks, sir."

Fielding pulled up a chair beside the bed. "I understand you've been debriefed about what happened?"

She nodded. "I will sign my statement when I get out of here."

Fielding nodded again. "I've read your statement. I know Chambers was more than your boss. He was your mentor. It occurred to me you must be struggling a bit with all of this."

She eyed him but remained silent. Was this him trying to drum her out of the ATF? Get her to quit? "It's difficult, I'll admit. I worked with John for a lot of years, and he was the best at what he did. Or at least he used to be. I guess not so much anymore."

"Yes, he was good. My understanding is that his debts and bitterness over his wife leaving him were what put him over the edge." Fielding steepled his fingers. "Sometimes good men go bad."

"Sounds like a country song," Piper blurted and then bit her lip. "Sorry. That just slipped out."

Fielding's smile was genuine. "You are not wrong. It does sound like a country song." He leaned deeper into his chair. "Agent Holloway... Piper, Chambers being crooked has left me in a quandary. I know that you, among others, thought I might be bent." She started to protest but he held up his hands. "John Chambers was nothing if not thorough. He planted a lot of seeds of doubt. The good thing is that my name does not appear on the thumb drive and that's gone a long way in restoring my reputation."

Piper brushed her hair out of her eyes. "They were able to decrypt it then?"

Fielding nodded. "Yes, and there are some very interesting names on it including Senator

Atlee, as Raider told us. It's going to take Washington a long time to clean up that mess."

Piper nodded. "I guess." She still wasn't sure where he was going with any of this.

"Agent Holloway… Piper, I know there were questions about how all this unfolded and you'll have to speak to the Office of Professional Responsibility and Security Affairs to get it all straight."

She braced herself for what was coming. He was firing her. She put her hands under the blanket and clutched at the sheet. "Yes, they've been in touch. We're supposed to meet next week."

"Good, good. Glad to hear it. As I was saying, once you've answered all OPR's questions then I would like you to think about what you'd like to do next."

Her stomach gave a lurch and sweat broke out across her palms. "Next, sir?"

"Yes." He leveled his steady gaze on her.

Piper took a deep breath and blew it out. "I've only ever wanted to be an ATF agent sir. Not sure what I will do if I'm…out."

Fielding frowned. "I think you misunderstood me. The ATF is grateful for all you did. You were a large part of the reason this operation was a success and you brought down a mole that, to be frank, we didn't know existed. You made us look golden when we could have been badly tarnished. What you did was a huge thing for the service."

Piper decided she might as well be frank. "I'm not following you, sir. Are you firing me?"

Fielding shook his head. "On the contrary, I'm offering you a promotion. I'd like you to run your own team."

She stared at him while what she wanted to do was jam her finger in her ear to be sure she was hearing okay. Was he being serious? "Really?" she asked her voice squeaking.

He smiled. "Yes, really. I hear through the grapevine that you have a bit of an impetuous nature. I understand it gets you into a bit of trouble now and then. You'll have to work on that."

She grinned. "Definitely."

Fielding's face clouded over again. "There is one thing."

Aw, shit. She'd known there had to be another shoe. The sound of it about to crash down accompanied the thudding of her heart.

She fisted the blankets once again. "And what would that be sir?

"With there being quite a few more people to arrest and lots of cases to sort out, it might be better if you didn't return to San Diego. A little time and distance would help keep you safer I think."

She stared at him. "You're worried about revenge."

He nodded once. "I think there are quite a few names on that list that scare me a bit. In your case I think it's a bit better if it's out of sight, out of mind. Just for a while until the dust settles."

"That's fine, sir." And it was. It was more than fine.

"Great," he said as he got to his feet. "Please let me know what office you want to work out of for the time being when you've made your choice."

"I will. Thank you, sir."

"Thank you, Agent Holloway," he said as he shook her hand and then promptly left the room.

Piper leaned back into the pillows and closed her eyes. She wasn't fired. It was a miracle. And she was getting a promotion. Her own team! How awesome was that? Except that the first person she wanted to share it with was Raider and even though he said he loved her, he'd walked away.

What had she expected? She'd lost their baby and kicked him out. It didn't matter that they loved each other. She'd destroyed everything.

She sunk into the pillows. Maybe Hawaii was the place to come. It would be far away from San Diego and all her past mistakes.

19

*R*aider sat back and admired the sunset. The eruption of Kilauea was doing some funky things to the sky, making the sunsets spectacular. He sipped his ice-cold beer. The bartender asked him if he wanted another, but he shook his head. He was taking it slow. He hadn't had much sleep and just wanted to sit and relax for a few minutes. The shower had been amazing and the bed was calling but he thought it might be nice to just watch the sunset and drink a beer before he slept for the next twenty hours.

"Hey," Harlan greeted him as he claimed the bar stool next to Raider.

"Hey yourself." He gave his friend the once over. "You look a little worse for wear but not too bad."

Harlan snorted. "I could say the same about you, except you look like shit."

"Thanks," Raider said sarcastically, but he knew his friend's assessment was spot on. He did look like shit. The shower helped but he needed some serious rack time. "Nothing twenty-four hours of sleep won't cure."

Harlan ordered a beer from the bartender. "You sure about that?"

Raider glanced at him in surprise. "What do you mean?"

"I mean, you just spent how many days with your ex-wife, whom you are still in love with, and discovered that she got pregnant and subsequently lost the baby. That's a whole lot of deep shit to work through. I'm thinking sleep isn't gonna be the answer to this one."

"I'm starting to regret telling you everything," Raider sniped.

"No, you're not," Harland said and then took a sip of his beer. He set the bottle on the bar. "You love me and are gagging for me to impart my wisdom." He smirked.

Raider let out a whoop of laughter. "Yeah, that's it. I'm hangin' on your every word, bro."

"Proper thing," Harlan shot back. Then the smile faded off his face. "Seriously, Raider, how are you doing?"

Raider shrugged. "I…I don't know. I mean,

fuck, on the one hand, I'm angry as hell at her. She should have told me about the pregnancy. She should've trusted me." He took a long swallow of his beer and then put the empty bottle on the bar. This time when the bartender came over he nodded his assent. He'd have just one more.

"And on the other hand?" Harlan countered.

"On the other hand, you're right. I still love her. I've never stopped loving her. Not even for a minute. Seeing her get shot damn near killed me. I don't want to be without her."

Harlan nodded. "It sucks to care about people because when shit happens to them, it's crippling."

The bottle was cold when Raider lifted his second beer to his lips. "You can say that again. Aged me twenty years."

"Makes you realize what Piper must have felt when you'd come back all busted up."

He stared at his friend. He'd never thought about it like that. He'd just assumed somehow it was different for her.

"So what are you gonna do?" Harlan pushed.

"No idea."

"That's bullshit. You know exactly what you're gonna do. You're just a puny little scaredy cat."

Raider turned to his best friend. "Did you just call me the name a five-year-old would use?"

"Uh-huh. Scaredy cat." Harlan tried to keep a

straight face but the two of them burst into laughter. "Finish your beer, get some sleep, and deal with it all in the morning. That's an order," he said as he clicked beer bottles with Raider.

"Yes, sir," Raider agreed. "Be happy to." All except the dealing with it in the morning. He wasn't happy about that at all.

Raider lurked just outside the hospital room door and watched as Piper signed the paperwork and handed it back to the nurse. She was ready to be discharged. He entered the room as the nurse finished giving Piper instructions on how to care for the wound.

"Thanks," Piper commented as the nurse bustled out of the room. She met Raider's gaze. Looking tired but a lot better than she had in the SUV, Piper offered him a small smile. "What brings you here?"

Raider cocked his head. "I think we need to talk."

Piper let out a long sigh. "I guess we do." She promptly sat down on the bed.

Raider stood a few feet away in the middle of the room. He didn't want to get any closer. This was hard enough as it was. The knot in his gut pained him. Each time he'd thought about all he had to say, his nerves jolted as though playing kickball with barbed wire. But he had to get all this out or it would haunt him for the rest of his days.

"Piper—"

"Raider—"

They both stared at each other. "You go first," he said as he crossed his arms over his chest.

She nodded. "Okay, I owe you an apology for how I treated you. I panicked about everything, losing the baby, Marta dying ... And instead of dealing with it, I took the easy route. I pushed you away. Somehow it was simpler to lock it all away if I didn't have to see you, see the disappointment in your face. I should have told you about the baby. I should've faced up to everything. I am so sorry for hiding it."

"I appreciate that." He stared at her and screwed up his courage. He needed to get this next part right. "Piper, I'm sorry too. Sorry we lost the baby, yeah, but also sorry I wasn't there to help you through that pain. I knew there was something more going on, but I didn't push. I should've fought harder."

She offered him a sad little smile. "Considering I was in a state of total denial, I'm not sure it would've made a difference. But thanks for saying it. If we're being honest then I should tell you that the real reason I didn't tell you about the baby was that if I said it out loud, if I told you, that made it real. You were still away and had two months left on your tour. I didn't think telling you over Facetime was the best way to let you know you were going to be a dad. Also, I was so terrified something would happen to you and I would end up raising our child on my own. I just don't think I could've done that. So, if I didn't tell you I was pregnant then the baby didn't really exist." She shook her head sadly. "Stupid, I know but I lived in terror of having a Navy Chaplain show up on my doorstep to tell me you were dead."

He sighed. "I get it. I really do. Seeing you get shot, well it almost destroyed me. I almost stopped functioning. I can't imagine what it was like for you waiting at home for me, never truly knowing what was going on with me. I understand your fear. I get why you didn't tell me. The part I have the hardest time with was that you didn't trust me enough to tell me after the fact what had happened. Why didn't you trust me, Piper?"

The ache in her heart made her want to ask the nurse for drugs, any drugs that would blot out the past. She rested a hand over her splintering heart. "I…I did trust you. I didn't trust me. I thought if I told you what I'd done, that I'd lost our baby by being reckless, you wouldn't love me anymore, that you'd hate me. I didn't think I could survive that, so I struck first. I thought if I drove you away then at least I would experience the pain of it all on my own terms. It was a form of…punishment, I guess. Penalizing myself for what happened." She wanted to reach out and touch him, but she kept her hands tightly laced together. "I'm just so sorry that I punished you as well."

Raider shook his head. "What happened could've happened to anyone and does every single damn day. Women miscarry all the time. Falling from the fence might have caused it or so might have a dozen other things. You shouldn't have blamed yourself. God knows I've made moves in the field that I look back on and realize how stupid they were. In the heat of battle, decision-making is different. I don't blame you for losing the baby. I'm just so pissed at you for not telling me. We've spent five long years apart because of it. What a waste."

She frowned at him. Her stomach fluttered. Was he saying…did he mean…

"What do you mean?"

"I mean I love you, Piper. I've loved you since that first night in the bar. I've never stopped loving you."

Excitement danced across her skin. Was he really taking her back? "I love you, too, Raider. I am so sorry for what I did. If you give me another chance I promise I will never push you away like that again."

Raider stared at her and then opened his arms. She got off the bed and walked into them. A wave of emotion rolled over her. She was home. The only home she'd ever really known. The only love she ever wanted.

Raider pulled back. "You've got to promise; No more secrets."

She smiled. "Deal."

He swooped down and captured her lips with a scorching kiss.

20

---

*R*aider leaned his elbows on the bar and watched Waylen and Kian play pool.

"Dude, you cheated," Kian yelled like a drama queen.

Waylen snorted. "I don't need to cheat to beat you."

"Yes, you do, and you know it. You suck at pool." Kian turned to Lane. "You saw that, didn't you?"

Lane merely shook his head. "I'm staying out of it."

The waitress came by and asked if they wanted anything else. They all shook their heads. Raider looked around the bar. "I like this place. Ohana. That means family, right?"

"Yup," Harlan commented as he set his beer down on the bar. "And I agree. This place is cool."

Raider looked around. Pool tables and a dart board anchored one end, and there was a small stage at the other end. A long wooden bar gleaming gold in the low lighting and was jammed with locals. The surfboards and Tiki masks on the wall just added to the ambiance. A loud burst of laughter came from the open-air side of the bar. It felt like…home.

"You know," Raider started, "Piper has to pick a place to go. Fielding promised her a team of her own but he wants her out of San Diego and preferably not on the east coast. She's thinking of staying here."

Waylen straightened from taking his shot. "You thinking of staying with her?"

Raider nodded. "I kind of like it here. There's a certain Zen to it."

"I know what you mean. It's growing on me too," Lane agreed.

Kian shrugged. "Maybe. I haven't really seen much besides the freakin' volcano. Would be nice to check out a beach or two. Even some of the other islands. I hear Maui is nice."

"They're all nice," Harlan said. "But they're in the middle of the freakin' ocean. You want to be all the way out here?"

It was a valid question, even from a Navy man. It was in the middle of nowhere in a sense.

"That's true," Raider agreed. "Not a whole lot of choice on things to do."

"What are you talking about?" Lane said. "There's beaches and mountains. Where else can you ski and swim on the same day?"

"Nowhere and you can't do that here either 'cause you suck at skiing," Waylen said and the guys all laughed. It was true Lane wasn't much of a skier.

"We could do some great SCUBA diving and snorkeling," Harlan commented.

"Fishing," Kian added.

Raider laughed. "Since when have you ever been able to sit still long enough to fish?"

"Word," Lane said with a snicker.

"So there are touristy things to do," Raider said, "but what would we do full-time? I gotta tell you, retirement sucks. I hate not being busy. If I learned anything on this trip it's that volcanoes are unpredictable and I hate being bored."

"We don't have to decide anything now. Let's just hang out for a bit longer and see how it all goes," Harlan advised. "If Piper wants to settle here then you can consider it."

Raider nodded and took a long pull of his beer.

"Are you two going to get married again?" Waylen asked as he moved the cue ball to better set up his shot.

"Er…not exactly."

"What does that mean, Raider?" Kian demanded.

"Well…I never signed the divorce papers."

"Say what?" Harlan stared at his friend. "You never signed them?"

Raider shook his head. He'd never been able to bring himself to do it.

"Holy shit!" Harlan started to laugh. "What are you gonna tell her when she starts talking about another wedding?"

Raider shrugged. "I'm gonna do my best to distract her."

Kian burst out laughing. "Good luck with that one, buddy. Women are all about the weddings."

He was not wrong. Raider knew at some point he'd have to tell Piper the truth but maybe he'd wait until she was over the moon happy first, and he had a few ideas on how to make her that way.

Brotherhood Protectors Hawaii World Team Koa Alpha

Lane Unleashed - Regan Black
Harlan Unleashed - Stacey Wilk
Raider Unleashed - Lori Matthews

Waylen Unleashed - Jen Talty
Kian Unleashed - Kris Norris

**Please be sure to visit my webpage to
follow me and keep up on my news.
https://lorimatthewsbooks.com**

Cease and Desist

Coast Guard Recon

Diverted

Incinerated

Conflicted

Subverted

Terminated

Coast Guard Hawai'i

A Lethal Betrayal

Free with Newsletter Sign Up

Falling For The Witness

Risk Assessment

Visit **Https://www.lorimatthewsbooks.com** for details on how to purchase these novels or sign up for my newsletter.

ABOUT THE AUTHOR

Lori Matthews grew up in a house filled with books and readers. She was introduced to different genres because of her parents' habit of leaving books all over the house. Her mother read romance, and her father read thrillers. Her love of reading and books led to her becoming a librarian. She started her career as a public librarian and then eventually made her way into schools as a high school librarian with a stop in the corporate world along the way.

When her children went off to school, she finally had the time to pursue her first love, writing and she's been pounding the keyboard ever since. She's won numerous writing awards including two Daphne Du Maurier awards. She currently lives in New Jersey with her husband, two children, her crazy dog, and her grumpy cat.

Follow me on social media by clicking the links below. And be sure to visit my webpage to keep up on my news. https://lorimatthewsbooks.com

Facebook: facebook.com/LoriMatthewsBooks

X (Twitter): x.com/_LoriMatthews_

Instagram: instagram.com/lorimatthewsbooks

Goodreads: goodreads.com/author/show/7733959.Lori_Matthews

Bookbub: bookbub.com/profile/lori-matthews

BROTHERHOOD PROTECTORS WORLD

ORIGINAL SERIES BY ELLE JAMES

Brotherhood Protectors Hawaii World

Team Koa Alpha

Lane Unleashed - Regan Black

Harlan Unleashed - Stacey Wilk

Raider Unleashed - Lori Matthews

Waylen Unleashed - Jen Talty

Kian Unleashed - Kris Norris

Brotherhood Protectors Yellowstone World

Team Wolf

Guarding Harper - - Desiree Holt

Guarding Hannah - Delilah Devlin

Guarding Eris - Reina Torres

Guarding Payton - Jen Talty

Guarding Leah - Regan Black

Team Eagle

Booker's Mission - Kris Norris

Hunter's Mission - Kendall Talbot

Gunn's Mission - Delilah Devlin

Xavier's Mission - Lori Matthews

Wyatt's Mission - Jen Talty

Corbin's Mission - Jen Talty

Tyson's Mission - Delilah Devlin

Knox's Mission - Barb Han

Colton's Mission - Kendall Talbot

Walker's Mission - Kris Norris

Brotherhood Protectors Colorado World

Team Watchdog

Mason's Watch - Jen Talty

Asher's Watch - Leanne Tyler

Cruz's Watch - Stacey Wilk

Kent's Watch- Deanna L. Rowley

Ryder's Watch- Kris Norris

Team Raptor

Darius' Promise - Jen Talty

Simon's Promise - Leanne Tyler

Nash's Promise - Stacey Wilk

Spencer's Promise - Deanna L. Rowley

Logan's Promise - Kris Norris

Team Falco

Fighting for Esme - Jen Talty

Fighting for Charli - Leanne Tyler

Fighting for Tessa - Stacey Wilk

Fighting for Kora - Deanna L. Rowley

Fighting for Fiona - Kris Norris

Athena Project

Beck's Six - Desiree Holt

Victoria's Six - Delilah Devlin

Cygny's Six - Reina Torres

Fay's Six - Jen Talty

Melody's Six - Regan Black

Team Trojan

Defending Sophie - Desiree Holt

Defending Evangeline - Delilah Devlin

Defending Casey - Reina Torres

Defending Sparrow - Jen Talty

Defending Avery - Regan Black

BROTHERHOOD PROTECTORS

ORIGINAL SERIES BY ELLE JAMES

Remy (#1)

Gerard (#2)

Lucas (#3)

Beau (#4)

Rafael (#5)

Valentin (#6)

Landry (#7)

Simon (#8)

Maurice (#9)

Jacques (#10)

Brotherhood Protectors

Montana SEAL's Mail-Order Bride (#12)

SEAL Justice (#13)

Ranger Creed (#14)

Delta Force Rescue (#15)

Dog Days of Christmas (#16)

Montana Rescue (#17)

Montana Ranger Returns (#18)

Hot SEAL Salty Dog (SEALs in Paradise)

Hot SEAL, Hawaiian Nights (SEALs in Paradise)

Hot SEAL Bachelor Party (SEALs in Paradise)

Hot SEAL, Independence Day (SEALs in Paradise)

Brotherhood Protectors Boxed Set 1

Brotherhood Protectors Boxed Set 2

Brotherhood Protectors Boxed Set 3

Brotherhood Protectors Boxed Set 4

Brotherhood Protectors Boxed Set 5

Brotherhood Protectors Boxed Set 6

ABOUT ELLE JAMES

ELLE JAMES also writing as MYLA JACKSON is a *New York Times* and *USA Today* Bestselling author of books including cowboys, intrigues and paranormal adventures that keep her readers on the edges of their seats. When she's not at her computer, she's traveling, snow skiing, boating, or riding her ATV, dreaming up new stories. Learn more about Elle James at www.ellejames.com

Website | Facebook | Twitter | GoodReads | Newsletter | BookBub | Amazon

Or visit her alter ego Myla Jackson at mylajackson.com
Website | Facebook | Twitter | Newsletter

Follow Me!
www.ellejames.com
ellejamesauthor@gmail.com